Juliana Horati

Six to Sixteen

outlook

Juliana Horatia Ewing

Six to Sixteen

1st Edition | ISBN: 978-3-73406-072-4

Place of Publication: Frankfurt am Main, Germany

Year of Publication: 2019

Outlook Verlag GmbH, Germany.

"'I've got a pink silk here,' said I, 'and pink shoes.'"

SIX TO SIXTEEN.

A STORY FOR GIRLS.

BY

JULIANA HORATIA EWING.

LONDON:
SOCIETY FOR PROMOTING CHRISTIAN KNOWLEDGE,
NORTHUMBERLAND AVENUE, W.C.
NEW YORK: E. & J. B. YOUNG & CO.

[Published under the direction of the General Literature Committee.]

DEDICATION.

TO MISS ELEANOR LLOYD.

MY DEAR ELEANOR,

I wish that this little volume were worthier of being dedicated to you.

It is, I fear, fragmentary as a mere tale, and cannot even plead as an excuse for this that it embodies any complete theory on the vexed question of the upbringing of girls. Indeed, I should like to say that it contains no attempt to paint a model girl or a model education, and was originally written as a sketch of domestic life, and not as a vehicle for theories.

That it does touch by the way on a few of the many strong opinions I have on the subject you will readily discover; though it is so long since we held discussions together that I hardly know how far your views will now agree with mine.

If, however, it seems to you to illustrate a belief in the joys and benefits of intellectual hobbies, I do not think that we shall differ on that point; and it may serve, here and there, to recall one, nearly as dear to you as to me, for whom the pleasures of life were at least doubled by such interests, and who found in them no mean resource under a burden heavier than common of life's pain.

That, whatever labour I may spend on this or any other bit of work—whatever changes or confirmations time and experience may bring to my views of people and things—I cannot now ask her approval of the one, or delight in the play of her strong intellect and bright wit over the other, is an unhealable sorrow with which no one sympathizes more fully than you.

This story was written before her death: it has been revised without her help.

Such as it is, I beg you to accept it in affectionate remembrance of old times and of many common hobbies of our girlhood in my Yorkshire home and in yours.

J. H. E.

SIX TO SIXTEEN.

INTRODUCTION.

Eleanor and I are subject to *fads*. Indeed, it is a family failing. (By the family I mean our household, for Eleanor and I are not, even distantly, related.) Life would be comparatively dull, up away here on the moors, without them. Our fads and the boys' fads are sometimes the same, but oftener distinct. Our present one we would not so much as tell them of on any account; because they would laugh at us. It is this. We purpose this winter to write the stories of our own lives down to the present date.

It seems an egotistical and perhaps silly thing to record the trivialities of our everyday lives, even for fun, and just to please ourselves. I said so to Eleanor, but she said, "Supposing Mr. Pepys had thought so about his everyday life, how much instruction and amusement would have been lost to the readers of his Diary." To which I replied, that as Mr. Pepys lived in stirring times, and amongst notable people, *his* daily life was like a leaf out of English history, and his case quite different to the case of obscure persons living simply and monotonously on the Yorkshire moors. On which Eleanor observed that the simple and truthful history of a single mind from childhood would be as valuable, if it could be got, as the whole of Mr. Pepys' Diary from the first volume to the last. And when Eleanor makes a general observation of this kind in her conclusive tone, I very seldom dispute it; for, to begin with, she is generally right, and then she is so much more clever than I.

One result of the confessed superiority of her opinion to mine is that I give way to it sometimes even when I am not quite convinced, but only helped by a little weak-minded reason of my own in the background. I gave way in this instance, not altogether to her argument (for I am sure *my* biography will not be the history of a mind, but only a record of small facts important to no one but myself), but chiefly because I think that as one grows up one enjoys recalling the things that happened when one was little. And one forgets them so soon! I envy Eleanor for having kept her childish diaries. I used to write diaries too, but, when I was fourteen years old, I got so much ashamed of them (it made me quite hot to read my small moral reflections, and the pompous account of my quarrels with Matilda, my sentimental admiration for the handsome bandmaster, &c., even when alone), and I was so afraid of the boys getting hold of them, that I made a big hole in the kitchen fire one day, and burned them all. At least, so I thought; but one volume escaped the flames, and the fun Eleanor and I have now in re-reading this has made me regret that I burned the others. Of course, even if I put down all that I can remember, it will not be like having kept my diaries. Eleanor's biography, in this respect, will be much better than mine; but still, I remember a good deal now that I dare say I shall forget soon, and in sixteen more years these histories may amuse us as much as the old diaries. We are all growing up now. We have even got to speaking of "old times," by which we mean the times when we used to wade in the brooks and——

But this is beside the mark, and I must not allow myself to wander off. I am too apt to be discursive. When I had to write leading articles for our manuscript periodical, Jack used to laugh at me, and say, "If it wasn't for Eleanor's disentangling your sentences, you'd put parenthesis within parenthesis till, when you got yourself into the very inside one, you'd be as puzzled as a pig in a labyrinth, and not know how to get back to where you started from." And I remember Clement—who generally disputed a point, if possible—said, "How do you know she wouldn't get back, if you let her work out each train of thought in peace? The curt, clean-cut French style may suit some people, whose brains won't stretch far without getting tired; but others may have more sympathy with a Semitic cast of mind."

This excuse pleased me very much. It was pleasanter to believe that my style was Semitic, than to allow, with Jack, that it tended towards that of Mrs. Nickleby. Though at that time my notion of the meaning of the word Semitic was not so precise as it might have been.

Our home is a beautiful place in the summer, and in much of spring and autumn. In winter I fancy it would look dreary to the eyes of strangers. At night the wind comes over the top of Deadmanstone Hill, and down the valley, whirls the last leaves off the old trees by the church, and sends them dancing over the closely-ranged gravestones. Then up through the village it comes, and moans round our house all night, like some miserable being wanting to get in. The boys say it does get in, more than enough, especially into their bedrooms; but then boys always grumble. It certainly makes strange noises here. I have more than once opened the back-door late in the evening, because I fancied that one of the dogs had been hurt, and was groaning outside.

That stormy winter after the Ladybrig murder, our fancies and the wind together played Eleanor and me sad tricks. When once we began to listen we seemed to hear a whole tragedy going on close outside. We could distinguish footsteps and voices through the bluster, and then a struggle in the shrubbery, and a *thud*, and a groan, and then a roar of wind, half drowning the sound of flying footsteps—and then an awful pause, and at last faint groaning, and a bump, as of some poor wounded body falling against the house. At this point we were wont to summon courage and rush out, with the kitchen poker and a candle shapeless with tallow shrouds from the strong draughts. We never could see anything; partly, perhaps, because the candle was always blown out; and when we stood outside it became evident that what we had heard was only the wind, and a bough of the old acacia-tree, which beat at intervals upon the house.

When the nights are stormy there is no room so comfortable as the big kitchen. We first used it for parochial purposes, small night-schools, and so forth. Then one evening, as we strolled in to look for one of the dogs, the cook said, "You can sit here, if you like, Miss Eleanor. *We* always sits in the pantry on winter nights; so there'll be no one to disturb you." And as we had some writing on hand which we did not wish to have discussed or overlooked by other members of the family, we settled down in great peace and comfort by the roaring fire which the maids had heaped to keep the kitchen warm in their absence.

We found ourselves so cosy and independent that we returned again and again to our new study. The boys (who go away a great deal more than we do, and are apt to come back dissatisfied with our "ways," and anxious to make us more "like other people") object strongly to this habit of ours. They say, "Who ever *heard* of ladies sitting in the kitchen?" And, indeed, there are many south-country kitchens in which I should not at all like to sit. But we have this large, airy, spotlessly clean room, with its stone floor, its yellow-washed walls, its tables scrubbed to snowy whiteness, its quaint old dresser and clock and corner cupboards of shiny black oak, and its huge fire-place and blazing fire all to ourselves, and we have abundance of room, and may do anything we please, so I think it is no wonder that we like it, though it be, in point of fact, a kitchen. We cover the table, and (commonly) part of the floor, with an amount of books, papers, and belongings of various sorts, such as we should scruple to deluge the drawing-room with. The fire crackles and blazes, so that we do not mind the wind, though there are no blinds to the kitchen, and if we do not "cotter" the shutters, we look out upon the black night, and the tall Scotch pine that has been tossed so wildly for so many years, and is not torn down yet.

Keziah the cook takes much pride in this same kitchen, which partly accounts for its being in a state so suitable to our use. She "stones" the floor with excruciating regularity. (At least, some people hate the scraping sound. I do not mind it myself.) She "pot-moulds" the hearth in fantastic patterns; the chests, the old chairs, the settle, the dresser, the clock and the corner cupboards are so many mirrors from constant polishing. She says, with justice, that "a body might eat his dinner off anything in the place."

We dine early, and the cooking for the late supper is performed in what we call "the second kitchen," beyond this. I believe that what is now the Vicarage was originally an old farmhouse, of which this same charming kitchen was the chief "living-room." It is quite a journey, through long, low passages, to get from the modern part of the house to this.

One year, when the "languages fad" was strong upon us, Eleanor and I earned many a backache by carrying the huge volumes of the *Della Crusca* Italian dictionary from the dining-room shelves to the kitchen. We piled them on the oak chest for reference, and ran backwards and forwards to them from the table where we sat and beat our brains over the "Divina Commedia," while the wind growled in the tall old box-trees without, and the dogs growled in dreams upon the hearth.

It is by this well-scrubbed table, in this kitchen, that our biographies are to be written. They cannot be penned under the noses of the boys.

Eleanor finds rocking a help to composition, and she is swinging backwards and forwards in the glossy old rocking-chair, with a pen between her lips, and a vacant gaze in her eyes, that becomes almost a look of inspiration when the swing of the chair turns her face towards the ceiling. For my own part I find that I can meet the crisis of a train of ideas best upon my feet, so I pace up and down past the old black dresser, with its gleaming crockery, like a captain on his quarter-deck. Suddenly Eleanor's chair stands still.

"Margery," she says, laying her head upon the table at her side, "I do think this is a capital idea."

"Yours will be capital," I reply, pausing also, and leaning back against the dresser; "for you have kept your old diaries, and——"

"My dear Margery, what if I have kept my old diaries? I've lived in this place my whole life. Now, you have had some adventures! I quite look forward to reading your life, Margery. You have no idea what pleasure it gives me to think of it. I was thinking just now, if ever we are separated in life, how I shall enjoy looking over it again and again. You must give me yours, you know, and I will give you mine. Yes; I am very glad we thought of it." And Eleanor begins to rock once more, and I resume my march.

But this quite settles the matter in my mind. To please Eleanor I would try to do a great deal; much more than this. I will write my autobiography.

Though it seems rather (to use an expressive Quaker term) a “need-not” to provide for our being separated in life, when we have so firmly resolved to be old maids, and to live together all our lives in the little whitewashed cottage behind the church.

CHAPTER I.

MY PRETTY MOTHER—AYAH—COMPANY.

My name is Margaret Vandaleur. My father was a captain in her Majesty's 202nd Regiment of Foot. The regiment was in India for six years, just after I was born; indeed, I was not many months old when I made my first voyage, which I fancy Eleanor is thinking of when she says that I have had some adventures.

Military ladies are said to be unlucky as to the times when they have to change stations; the move often chancing at an inconvenient moment. My mother had to make her first voyage with the cares of a young baby on her hands; nominally, at any rate, but I think the chief care of me fell upon our Ayah. My mother hired her in England. The Ayah wished to return to her country, and was glad to do so as my nurse. I think that at first she only intended to be with us for the voyage, but she stayed on, and became fond of me, and so remained my nurse as long as I was in India.

I have heard that my mother was the prettiest woman on board the vessel she went out in, and the prettiest woman at the station when she got there. Some people have told me that she was the prettiest woman they ever saw. She was just eighteen years old when my father married her, and she was not six-and-twenty when she died.

[I got so far in writing my life, seated at the round, three-legged pinewood table, with Eleanor scribbling away opposite to me. But I could get no further just then. I put my hands before my eyes as if to shade them from the light; but Eleanor is very quick, and she found out that I was crying. She jumped up and threw herself at my feet.

"Margery, dear Margery! what *is* the matter?"

I could only sob, "My mother, O my mother!" and add, almost bitterly, "It is very well for you to write about your childhood, who have had a mother —and such a mother!—all your life; but for me——"

Eleanor knelt straight up, with her teeth set, and her hands clasped before her.

"I do think," she said slowly, "that I am, without exception, the most selfish, inconsiderate, dense, unfeeling brute that ever lived." She looked so quaintly, vehemently in earnest as she knelt in the firelight, that I laughed in spite of my tears.

“My dear old thing,” I said, “it is I who am selfish, not you. But I am going on now, and I promise to disturb you no more.” And in this I was resolute, though Eleanor would have burned our papers then and there, if I had not prevented her.

Indeed she knew as well as I did that it was not merely because I was an orphan that I wept, as I thought of my early childhood. We could not speak of it, but she knew enough to guess at what was passing through my mind. I was only six years old when my mother died, but I can remember her. I can remember her brief appearances in the room where I played, in much dirt and contentment, at my Ayah’s feet—rustling in silks and satins, glittering with costly ornaments, beautiful and scented, like a fairy dream. I would forego all these visions for one—only one—memory of her praying by my bedside, or teaching me at her knee. But she was so young, and so pretty! And yet, O Mother, Mother! better than all the triumphs of your loveliness in its too short prime would it have been to have left a memory of your beautiful face with some devout or earnest look upon it—“as it had been the face of an angel”—to your only child.

As I sit thinking thus, I find Eleanor’s dark eyes gazing at me from her place, to which she has gone back; and she says softly, “Margery, dear Margery, do let us give it up.” But I would not give it up now, for anything whatever.]

The first six years of my life were spent chiefly with my Ayah. I loved her very dearly. I kissed and fondled her dark cheeks as gladly as if they had been fair and ruddy, and oftener than I touched my mother’s, which were like the petals of a china rose. My most intimate friends were of the Ayah’s complexion. We had more than one “bearer” during those years, to whom I was greatly attached. I spoke more Hindostanee than English. The other day I saw a group of Lascar sailors at the Southampton Station; they had just come off a ship, and were talking rapidly and softly together. I have forgotten the language of my early childhood, but its tones had a familiar sound; those dark bright faces were like the faces of old friends, and my heart beat for a minute, as one is moved by some remembrance of an old home.

When my mother went out for her early ride at daybreak, before the heat of the day came on, Ayah would hold me up at the window to see her start. Sometimes my father would have me brought out, and take me before him on his horse for a few minutes. But my nurse never allowed this if a ready excuse could prevent it. Her care of me was maternal in its tenderness, but she did not keep me tidy enough for me to be presentable off-hand to company.

There was always “company” wherever my mother went—gentleman company especially. The gentlemen, in different places, and at different times, were not the same, but they had a common likeness. I used to count them when they rode home with my father and mother, or assembled for any of the many reasons for which "company" hung about our homes. I remember that it was an amusement to me to discover, "there are six to-day," or "five to-day," and to tell my Ayah. I was even more minute. I divided them into three classes: "the little ones, the middle ones, and the old ones." The "little ones" were the very young men—smooth-cheeked ensigns, etc.; the "old ones" were usually colonels, generals, or elderly civilians. From the youngest to the oldest, officers and civilians, they were all very good-natured to me, and I approved of them accordingly.

When callers came, I was often sent into the drawing-room. Great was my dear Ayah's pride when I was dressed in pink silk, my hair being arranged in ringlets round my head, to be shown off to the company. I was proud of myself, and was wont rather to strut than walk into the room upon my best kid shoes. They were pink, to match my frock, and I was not a little vain of them. There were usually some ladies in the room, dressed in rustling finery like my mother, but not like her in the face—never so pretty. There were always plenty of gentlemen of the three degrees, and they used to be very polite to me, and to call me "little Rosebud," and give me sweetmeats. I liked sweetmeats, and I liked flattery, but I had an affection stronger than my fancy for either. I used to look sharply over the assembled men for the face I wanted, and when I had found it I flew to the arms that were stretched out for me. They were my father's.

I remember my mother, but I remember my father better still. I did not see very much of him, but when we were together I think we were both thoroughly happy. I can recall pretty clearly one very happy holiday we spent together. My father got some leave, and took us for a short time to the hills. My clearest memory of his face is as it smiled on me, from under a broad hat, as we made nosegays for Mamma's vases in our beautiful garden, where the fuchsias and geraniums were "hardy," and the sweet-scented verbenas and heliotropes were great bushes, loading the air with perfume.

I have one remembrance of it almost as distinct—the last.

CHAPTER II.

THE CHOLERA SEASON—MY MOTHER GOES AWAY—MY SIXTH BIRTHDAY.

We were living in a bungalow not far from the barracks at X. when the cholera came. It was when I was within a few weeks of six years old. First we heard that it was among the natives, and the matter did not excite much notice. Then it broke out among the men, and the officers talked a good deal about it. The next news was of the death of the Colonel commanding our regiment.

One of my early recollections is of our hearing of this. An ensign of our regiment (one of the "little ones") called upon my mother in the evening of the day of the Colonel's death. He was very white, very nervous, very restless. He brought us the news. The Colonel had been ill barely thirty-six hours. He had suffered agonies with wonderful firmness. He was to be buried the next day.

"He never was afraid of cholera," said Mr. Gordon; "he didn't believe it was infectious; he thought keeping up the men's spirits was everything. But, you see, it isn't nervousness, after all, that does it."

"It goes a long way, Gordon," said my father. "You're young; you've never been through one of these seasons. Don't get fanciful, my good fellow. Come here, and play with Margery."

Mr. Gordon laughed.

"I am a fool, certainly," he said. "Ever since I heard of it, I have fancied a strange, faint kind of smell everywhere, which is absurd enough."

"I will make you a camphor-bag," said my mother, "that ought to overpower any faint smell, and it is a charm against infection."

I believe Mr. Gordon was beginning to thank her, but his words ended in a sort of inarticulate groan. He stood on his feet, though not upright, and at last said feebly, "I beg your pardon, I don't feel quite well."

"You're upset, old fellow; it's quite natural," said my father. "Come and get some brandy, and you shall come back for the camphor."

My father led him away, but he did not come back. My father took him to his quarters, and sent the surgeon to him; and my mother took me on her knee, and sat silent for a long time, with the unfinished camphor-bag beside her.

The next day I went to the end of our compound with Ayah, to see the Colonel's funeral pass. The procession seemed endless. The horse he had ridden two days before by my mother's side tossed its head fretfully, as the "Dead March" wailed, and the slow tramp of feet poured endlessly on. My mother was looking out from the verandah. As Ayah and I joined her, a native servant, who was bringing something in, said abruptly, "Gordon Sahib—he dead too."

When my father returned from the funeral he found my mother in a panic. Some friends had lately invited her to stay with them, and she was now resolved to go. "I am sure I shall die if I stay here!" she cried, and it ended in her going away at once. There was some difficulty as to accommodating me and Ayah, and it was decided that, if necessary, we should follow my mother later.

For my own part, I begged to remain. I had no fear of cholera, and I was anxious to dine with my father on my birthday, as he had promised that I should.

It was on the day before my birthday that one of the surgeons was buried. The man next in rank to the poor Colonel was on leave, and the regiment was commanded by our friend Major Buller, whose little daughters were invited to spend the following evening with me. The Major, my father, and two other officers had been pall-bearers at the funeral. My father came to me on his return. He was slightly chilled, and said he should remain indoors; so I had him all to myself, and we were very happy, though he complained of fatigue, and fell asleep once on the floor with his head in my lap. He was still lying on the floor when Ayah took me to bed. I believe he had been unwell all the day, though I did not know it, and had been taking some of the many specifics against cholera, of which everybody had one or more at that time.

Half-an-hour later he sent for a surgeon, who happened to be dining with Major Buller. The Doctor and the Major came together to our bungalow, and with them two other officers who happened to be of the party, and who were friends of my father. One of them was a particular friend of my own. He was an ensign, a reckless, kind-hearted lad "in his teens," a Mr. Abercrombie, who had good reason to count my father as a friend.

Mr. Abercrombie mingled in some way with my dreams that night, or rather early morning, and when I fairly woke, it was to the end of a discussion betwixt my Ayah, who was crying, and Mr. Abercrombie, in evening dress, whose face bore traces of what looked to me like crying also. I was hastily clothed, and he took me in his arms.

"Papa wants you, Margery dear," he said; and he carried me quickly down the passages in the dim light of the early summer dawn.

Two or three officers, amongst whom I recognized Major Buller, fell back, as we came in, from the bed to which Mr. Abercrombie carried me. My father turned his face eagerly towards me, but I shrank away. That one night of suffering and collapse had changed him so that I did not know him again. At last I was persuaded to go to him, and by his voice and manner recognized him as his feeble fingers played tenderly with mine. And when he said, "Kiss me, Margery dear," I crept up and kissed his forehead, and started to feel it so cold and damp.

"Be a good girl, Margery dear," he whispered; "be very good to Mamma." There was a short silence. Then he said, "Is the sun rising yet, Buller?"

"Just rising, old fellow. Does the light bother you?"

"No, thank you; I can't see it. The fact is, I can't see you now. I suppose it's nearly over. GOD's will be done. You've got the papers, Buller? Arkwright will be kind about it, I'm sure. You'll break it to my wife as well as you can?"

After another pause he said, "It's time you fellows went to bed and got some sleep."

But no one moved, and there was another silence, which my father broke by saying, "Buller, where are you? It's quite dark now. Would you say the Lord's Prayer for me, old fellow? Margery dear, put your hands with poor Papa's."

"I've not said my prayers yet," said I; "and you know I ought to say my prayers, for I've been dressed a long time."

The Major knelt simply by the bed. The other men, standing, bent their heads, and Mr. Abercrombie, kneeling, buried his face on the end of the bed and sobbed aloud.

Major Buller said the Lord's Prayer. I, believing it to be my duty, said it also, and my father said it with us to the clause "For Thine is the kingdom, the power, and the glory," when his voice failed, and I, thinking he had forgotten (for I sometimes forgot in the middle of my most familiar prayers and hymns), helped him—"Papa dear! *for ever and ever*."

Still he was silent, and as I bent over him I heard one long-drawn breath, and then his hands, which were enfolded with mine, fell apart. The sunshine was now beginning to catch objects in the room, and a ray lighted up my father's face, and showed a change that even I could see. An officer standing at the head of the bed saw it also, and said abruptly, "He's dead, Buller." And the Major, starting up, took me in his arms, and carried me away.

I cried and struggled. I had a dim sense of what had happened, mixed with an idea that these men were separating me from my father. I could notbe pacified till Mr. Abercrombie held out his arms for me. He was more like a woman, and he was crying as well as I. I went to him and buried my sobs on his shoulder. Mr. George (as I had long called him, from finding his surname hard to utter) carried me into the passage and walked up and down, comforting me.

"Is Papa really dead?" I at length found voice to ask.

"Yes, Margery dear. I'm so sorry."

"Will he go to Abraham's bosom, Mr. George?"

"Will he go *where*, Margery?"

"To Abraham's bosom, you know, where the poor beggar went that's lying on the steps in my Sunday picture-book, playing with those dear old dogs."

Mr. Abercrombie's knowledge of Holy Scripture was, I fear, limited. Possibly my remarks recalled some childish remembrance similar to my own. He said, "Oh yes, to be sure. Yes, dear."

"Do you think the dogs went with the poor beggar?" I asked. "Do you think the angels took them too?"

"I don't know," said Mr. George. "I hope they did."

There was a pause, and then I asked, in awe-struck tones, "Will the angels fetch Papa, do you think?"

Mr. George had evidently decided to follow my theological lead, and he replied, "Yes, Margery dear."

"Shall you see them?" I asked.

"No, no, Margery. I'm not good enough to see angels."

"*I* think you're very good," said I. "And please be good, Mr. George, and then the angels will fetch you, and perhaps me, and Mamma, and perhaps Ayah, and perhaps Bustle, and perhaps Clive." Bustle was Mr. Abercrombie's dog, and Clive was a mastiff, the dog of the regiment, and a personal friend of mine.

"Very well, Margery dear. And now you must be good too, and you must let me take you to bed, for it's morning now, and I have had no sleep at all."

"Is it to-morrow now?" I asked; "because, if it's to-morrow, it's my birthday." And I began to cry afresh, because Papa had promised that I should dine with him, and had promised me a present also.

"I'll give you a birthday present," said my long-suffering friend; and he began to unfasten a locket that hung at his watch-chain. It was of Indian gold, with forget-me-nots in turquoise stones upon it. He opened it and pulled out a photograph, which he tore to bits, and then trampled underfoot.

"There, Margery, there's a locket for you; you can throw it into the fire, or do anything you like with it. And I wish you many happy returns of the day." And he finally fastened it round my neck with his Trichinopoli watch-chain, leaving his watch loose in his waistcoat-pocket. The locket and chain pleased me, and I suffered him to carry me to bed. Then, as he was parting from me, I thought of my father again, and asked:

"Do you think the angels have fetched Papa *now*, Mr. George?"

"I think they have, Margery."

Whereupon I cried myself to sleep. And this was my sixth birthday.

CHAPTER III.

THE BULLERS—MATILDA TAKES ME UP—WE FALL OUT—MR. GEORGE.

Major Buller took me home to his house after my father's death. My father had left his affairs in his hands, and in those of a friend in England—the Mr. Arkwright he had spoken of. I believe they were both trustees under my mother's marriage settlement.

The Bullers were relations of mine. Mrs. Buller was my mother's cousin. She was a kind-hearted, talkative lady, and good-looking, though no longer very young. She dressed as gaily as my poor mother, though, somehow, not with quite so good an effect. She copied my mother's style, and sometimes wore things exactly similar to hers; but the result was not the same. I have heard Mrs. Minchin say that my mother took a malicious pleasure, at times, in wearing costumes that would have been most trying to beauty less radiant and youthful than hers, for the fun of seeing "poor Theresa" appear in a similar garb with less success. But Mrs. Minchin's tales had always a sting in them!

Mrs. Buller received me very kindly. She kissed me, and told me to call her "Aunt Theresa," which I did ever afterwards. Aunt Theresa's daughters and I were like sisters. They showed me their best frocks, and told me exactly all that had been ordered in the parcel that was coming out from England.

"Don't you have your hair put in papers?" said Matilda, whose own curls sat stiffly round her head as regularly as the rolls of a lawyer's wig. "Are your socks like lace? Doesn't your Ayah dress you every afternoon?"

Matilda "took me up." She was four years older than I was, which entitled her to blend patronage with her affection for me. In the evening of the day on which I went to the Bullers, she took me by the hand, and tossing her curls said, "I have taken you up, Margery Vandaleur. Mrs. Minchin told Mamma that she has taken the bride up. I heard her say that the bride was a sweet little puss, only so childish. That's just what Mrs. Minchin said. I heard her. And I shall say so of you, too, as I've taken you up. You're a sweet little puss. And of course you're childish, because you're a child," adds Miss Matilda, with an air. For had not she begun to write her own age with two figures?

Had I known then as much as I learned afterwards of what it meant to be "taken up" by Mrs. Minchin, I might not have thought the comparison a good omen for my friendship with Matilda. To be hotly taken up by Mrs. Minchin meant an equally hot quarrel at no very distant date. The squabble with the bride was not slow to come, but Matilda and I fell out first. I think she was tyrannical, and I know I was peevish. My Ayah spoilt me; I spoke very broken English, and by no means understood all that the Bullers said to me; besides which, I was feverishly unhappy at intervals about my father.

It was two months before Mrs. Minchin found out that her sweet little puss was a deceitful little cat; but at the end of two days I had offended Matilda, and we plunged into a war of words such as children wage when they squabble.

"I won't show you any more of my dresses," said Matilda.

"I've seen them all," I boldly asserted; and the stroke told.

"You don't know that," said Matilda.

"Yes, I do."

"No, you don't."

"Well, show me the others then."

"No, that I won't."

"I don't care."

"I've got a blue silk coming out from England," Matilda continued, "but you haven't."

"I've got a pink silk here," said I, "and pink shoes."

"Ah, but you can't wear them now your papa's dead," said Matilda; "Mamma says you will have to wear black for twelve months."

I am sure Matilda did not mean to be cruel, but this blow cut me deeply. I remember the tide of misery that seemed to flood over my mind, to this day. I was miserable because my father was dead, and I could not go to him for comfort. I was miserable because I was out of temper, and Matilda had had the best of the quarrel. I was miserable—poor little wretch!—because I could not wear my pink silk, now my father was dead. I put my hands to my eyes, and screaming, "Papa! Papa!" I rushed out into the verandah.

As I ran out, some one ran in; we struck against each other, and Bustle and I rolled over on to the floor. In a moment more I was in Mr. Abercrombie's arms, and sobbing out my woes to him.

I am sorry to say that he swore rather loudly when he heard what Matilda had said, and I fancy that he lectured her when I had gone to Ayah, for she came to me presently and begged my pardon. Of course we were at once as friendly as before. Many another breach was there between us after that, hastily made and quickly healed. But the bride and Mrs. Minchin never came to terms.

"Mr. George" remained my devoted friend. I looked for him as I used to look for my father. The first time I saw him after I came to the Bullers was on the day of my father's funeral. He was there, and came back with Major Buller. I was on Mr. George's knee in a moment, with my hand through the crape upon his sleeve. The Major slowly unfastened his sword-belt, and laid it down with a sigh, saying, "We've lost a good man, Abercrombie, and a true friend."

"You don't know what a friend to me," said Mr. George impetuously. "Why, look here, sir. A month or two ago I'd outrun the constable—I always am getting into a mess of some sort—and Vandaleur found it out and lent me the money."

"You're not the first youngster he has helped by many, to my knowledge," said Major Buller.

"But that's not all, sir," said Mr. George, standing up with me in his arms. "When we first went in that night, you remember his speaking privately to me once? Well, what he said was, 'I think I'm following the rest, Abercrombie, and I wanted to speak to you about this.' He had got my I.O.U. in his hand, and he tore it across, and said, 'Don't bother any more about it; but keep straight, my boy, if you can, for your people's sake.' I'm sadly given to going crooked, sir, but if anything could make a fellow——"

Mr. George got no further in his sentence, but the Major seemed to understand what he meant, for he spoke very kindly to him, and they left me for a bit and walked up and down the verandah together. Just before Mr. George left, I heard him say, "Have you heard anything of Mrs. Vandaleur?"

"I wrote to her, in the best fashion that I could," said Major Buller. "But there's no breaking rough news gently, Abercrombie. I ought to hear from her soon."

But he never did hear from her. My poor mother had fled from the cholera only to fall a victim to fever. The news of my father's death was, I believe, the immediate cause of the relapse in which she died.

And so I became an orphan.

Shortly afterwards the regiment was ordered home, and the Bullers took me with them.

CHAPTER IV.

SALES—MATTERS OF PRINCIPLE—MRS. MINCHIN QUARRELS WITH THE BRIDE—MRS. MINCHIN QUARRELS WITH EVERYBODY —MRS. MINCHIN IS RECONCILED—THE VOYAGE HOME—A DEATH ON BOARD.

I only remember a little of our voyage home in the troop-ship, but I have heard so much of it, from the elder Buller girls and the ladies of the regiment, that I seem quite familiar with all that happened; and I hardly know now what I remember myself, and what has been recalled or suggested to me by hearing the other ladies talk.

There was no lack of subjects for talk when the news came that the regiment was ordered home. As Aunt Theresa repeatedly remarked, "There are a great many things to be considered." And she considered them all day long—by word of mouth.

The Colonel (that is, the new Colonel)—he had just returned from leave in the hills—and his wife behaved rather shabbily, it was thought. "But," as Mrs. Minchin said, "what could you expect? They say she was the daughter of a wholesale draper in the City. And trade in the blood always peeps out." We knew for certain that before there was a word said about the regiment going home, it had been settled that the Colonel's wife should go to England, where her daughters were being educated, and take the two youngest children with her. Her passage in the mail-steamer was all but taken, if not quite. And then, when they heard of the troop-ship, she stayed to go home in that. "Money can be no object to them," said Mrs. Minchin, "for one of the City people belonging to her has died lately, and left her—I can't tell you how many thousands. Indeed, they've heaps of money, and now he's got the regiment he ought to retire. And I must say, I think it's very hard on you, dear Mrs. Buller. With all your family, senior officer's wife's accommodation would be little enough, for a long voyage."

"Which is no reason why my wife should have better accommodation than she is entitled to, more than any other lady on board," observed Uncle Buller. "The Quartermaster's wife has more children than we have, and you know how much room she will get."

"Quartermaster's wife!" muttered Mrs. Minchin. "She would have been accommodated with the women of the regiment if we had gone home three months ago (at which time Quartermaster Curling was still only a sergeant)."

Uncle Buller made no reply. He was not fond of Mrs. Minchin, and he never disputed a point with her.

One topic of the day was "sales." We all had to sell off what we did not want to take home, and the point was to choose the right moment for doing so.

"I shan't be the first," said Aunt Theresa decidedly. "The first sales are always failures somehow. People are depressed. Then they know that there are plenty more to come, and they hang back. But further on, people have just got into an extravagant humour, and would go bargain-hunting to fifty sales a day. Later still, they find out that they've got all they want."

"And a great deal that they don't want," put in Uncle Buller.

"Which is all the same thing," said Aunt Theresa. "So I shall sell about the middle." Which she did, demanding her friends' condolences beforehand on the way in which her goods and chattels would be "given away," and receiving their congratulations afterwards upon the high prices that they fetched.

To do Aunt Theresa justice, if she was managing, she was quite honest.

[Eleanor is shocked by some of the things I say about people in our own rank of life. She believes that certain vulgar vices, such as cheating, lying, gluttony, petty gossip, malicious mischief-making, etc., are confined to the lower orders, or, as she wisely and kindly phrases it, to people who know no better. She laughs at me, and I laugh at myself, when I say (to support my own views) that I know more of the world than she does; since what I know of the world beyond this happy corner of it I learned when I was a mere child. But though we laugh, I can remember a good deal. I have heard polished gentlemen lie, at a pinch, like the proverbial pick-pocket, and pretty ladies fib as well as servant-girls. Of course, I do not mean to say that as many ladies as servant-girls tell untruths. But Eleanor would fain believe that the lie which Solomon discovered to be "continually on the lips of the untaught" is not on the lips of those who "know better" at all. As to dishonesty, too, I should be sorry to say that customers cheat as much as shopkeepers, but I do think that many people who ought to "know better" seem to forget that their honour as well as their interest is concerned in every bargain. The question then arises, do people in our rank know so much better on these points of moral conduct than those below them? If Eleanor and her parents are "old-fashioned" (and the boys think us quite behind the times), I fancy, that perhaps high principle and a nice sense of honour are not so well taught now as they used to be. Noble sentiments are not the fashion. The very phrase provokes a smile of ridicule. But I do not know whether the habit of uttering ignoble ones in "chaff" does not at last bring the tone of mind down to the low level. It is so terribly easy to be mean, and covetous, and selfish, and cowardly untrue, if the people by whose good opinion one's character lives will comfortably confess that they also "look out for themselves," and "take care of Number One," and think "money's the great thing in this world," and hold "the social lie" to be a necessary part of social intercourse. I know that once or twice it has happened that young people with whom we have been thrown have said things which have made high-principled Eleanor stand aghast in honourable horror; and that that speechless indignation of hers has been as much lost upon them as the touch of a feather on the hide of a rhinoceros. Eleanor is more impatient than I am on such subjects. I who have been trained in more than one school myself, am sorry for those who have never known the higher teaching. Eleanor thinks that modesty, delicacy of mind and taste, and uprightness in word and deed, are innate in worthy characters. Where she finds them absent, she is apt to dilate her nostrils, and say, in that low, emphatic voice which is her excited tone, "There are some things that you cannot *put into* anybody!" and so turn her back for ever on the offender. Or, as she once said to a friend of the boys, who was staying with us, in the heat of argument, "I supposed that honourable men, like poets, are born, not made." I, indeed, do believe these qualities to be in great measure inherited; but I believe them also to come of training, and to be more easily lost than Eleanor will allow. She has only lived in one moral atmosphere. I think that the standard of a family or a social circle falls but too easily; and in all humbleness of mind, I say that I have reason to believe that in this respect, as in other matters, elevation and amendment are possible.

However, this is one of the many subjects we discuss, rocking and pacing the kitchen to the howling of the wind. We have confessed that our experience is very small, and our opinions still unfixed in the matter, so it is unlikely that I shall settle it to my own, or anybody's satisfaction, in the pages of this biography.]

To return to Aunt Theresa. She was, as I said, honest. She chose a good moment for our sale; but she did not "doctor" the things. For the credit of the regiment, I feel ashamed to confess that everybody was not so scrupulous. One lady sat in our drawing-room, with twenty-five pounds' worth of lace upon her dress, and congratulated herself on having sold some toilette-china as sound, of which she had daintily doctored two fractures with an invaluable cement. The pecuniary gain may have been half-a-crown. The loss in self-respect she did not seem to estimate. Aunt Theresa would not have done it herself, but she laughed encouragingly. It is difficult to be strait-laced with a lady who had so much old point, and whose silks are so stiff that she can rustle down your remonstrances. Another friend, a young officer whose personal extravagance was a proverb even at a station in India, boasted for a week of having sold a rickety knick-knack shelf to a man who was going off to the hills for five-and-twenty rupees when it was not worth six. I have heard him swear at tailors, servants, and subordinates of all kinds, for cheating. I do not think it ever dawned upon his mind that common honesty was a virtue in which he himself was wanting. As to Mrs. Minchin's tales on this subject—but Mrs. Minchin's tales were not to be relied upon.

It was about this time that Mrs. Minchin and the bride quarrelled. In a few weeks after her arrival, the bride knew all the ladies of the regiment and the society of the station, and then showed little inclination to be bear-led by Mrs. Minchin. She met that terrible lady so smartly on one occasion that she retired, worsted, for the afternoon, and the bride drove triumphantly round the place, and called on all her friends, looking as soft as a Chinchilla muff, and dropping at every bungalow the tale of something that Mrs. Minchin had said, by no means to the advantage of the inmates.

It was in this way that Aunt Theresa came to know what Mrs. Minchin had said about her wearing half-mourning for my father and mother. That she knew better than to go into deep black, which is trying to indefinite complexions, but was equal to any length of grief in those lavenders, and delicate combinations of black and white, which are so becoming to everybody, especially to people who are not quite so young as they have been.

In the warmth of her own indignation at these unwarrantable remarks, and of the bride's ready sympathy, Aunt Theresa felt herself in candour bound to reveal what Mrs. Minchin had told her about the bride's having sold a lot of her wedding presents at the sale for fancy prices; they being new-fashioned ornaments, and so forth, not yet to be got at the station.

The result of this general information all round was, of course, a quarrel between Mrs. Minchin and nearly every lady in the regiment. The bride had not failed to let "the Colonel's lady" know what Mrs. Minchin thought of her going home in the troop-ship, and had made a call upon the Quartermaster's wife for the pleasure of making her acquainted with Mrs. Minchin's warm wish that the regiment had been ordered home three months sooner, when Mrs. Curling and the too numerous little Curlings would not have been entitled to intrude upon the ladies' cabin.

And yet, strange to say, before we were half-way to England, Mrs. Minchin was friendly once more with all but the bride; and the bride was at enmity with every lady on board. The truth is, Mrs. Minchin, though a gossip of the deepest dye, was kind-hearted, after a fashion. Her restless energy, which chiefly expended itself in petty social plots, and the fomentation of quarrels, was not seldom employed also in practical kindness towards those who happened to be in favour with her. She was really interested—for good or for evil—in those with whose affairs she meddled, and if she was a dangerous enemy, and a yet more dangerous friend, she was neither selfish nor illiberal.

The bride, on the other hand, had no real interest whatever in anybody's affairs but her own, and combined in the highest degree those qualities of personal extravagance and general meanness which not unfrequently go together.

A long voyage is no small test of temper; and it was a situation in which Mrs. Minchin's best qualities shone. It was proportionably unfavourable to those of the bride. Her maid was sick, and she was slovenly. She was sick herself, and then her selfishness and discontent knew no check. The other ladies bore their own little troubles, and helped each other; but under the peevish egotism of the bride, her warmest friends revolted. It was then that Mrs. Minchin resumed her sway amongst us.

With Aunt Theresa she was soon reconciled. Mrs. Buller's memory was always hazy, both in reference to what she said herself, and to what was said to her. She was too good-natured to strain it to recall past grievances. Her indignation had not lasted much beyond that afternoon in which the bride scattered discord among her acquaintances. She had relieved herself by outpouring the tale of Mrs. Minchin's treachery to Uncle Buller, and then taking him warmly to task for the indifference with which he heard her wrongs; and had ended by laughing heartily when he compared the probable encounter between Mrs. Minchin and the bride to the deadly struggles of two quarrelsome "praying-mantises" in his collection.

[Major Buller was a naturalist, and took home some rare and beautiful specimens of Indian insects.]

It was an outbreak of sickness amongst the little Curlings which led to the reconciliation with the Quartermaster's wife. Neither her kindness of heart nor her love of managing other folks' matters would permit Mrs. Minchin to be passive then. She made the first advances, and poor Mrs. Curling gratefully responded.

"I'm sure, Mrs. Minchin," said she, "I don't wonder at any one thinking the children would be in the way, poor dears. But of course, as Curling said——"

"God bless you, my good woman," Mrs. Minchin broke in. "Don't let us go back to that. We all know pretty well what Mrs. Seymour's made of, now. Let's go to the children. I'm as good a sick-nurse as most people, and if you keep up your heart we'll pull them all through before we get to the Cape."

But with all her zeal (and it did not stop short of a quarrel with the surgeon) and all her devotion, which never slackened, Mrs. Minchin did not "pull them all through."

We were just off the Cape when Arthur Curling died. He was my own age, and in the beginning of the voyage we had been playfellows. Of all the children who swarmed on deck to the distraction of (at least) the unmarried officers of the regiment, he had been the noisiest and the merriest. He made fancy ships in corners, to which he admitted the other children as fancy passengers, or fancy ship's officers of various grades. Once he employed a dozen of us to haul at a rope as if we were "heaving the log." Owing to an unexpected coil, it slackened suddenly, and we all fell over one another at the feet of two young officers who were marching up and down, arm-in-arm, absorbed in conversation. Their anger was loud as well as deep, but it did not deter Arthur Curling from further exploits, or stop his ceaseless chatter about what he would do when he was a man and the captain of a vessel.

He did not live to be either the one or the other. Some very rough weather off the Cape was fatal to him at a critical point in his illness. How Mrs. Minchin contrived to keep her own feet and to nurse the poor boy as she did was a marvel. He died on her knees.

The weather had been rough up to the time of his death, but it was a calm lovely morning on which his body was committed to the deep. The ship's bell tolled at daybreak, and all the ladies but the bride were with poor Mrs. Curling at the funeral. Mrs. Seymour lay in her berth, and whined complaints of "that horrid bell." She displayed something between an interesting terror and a shrewish anger because there was "a body on board." When she said that the Curlings ought to be thankful to have one child less to provide for, the other ladies hurried indignantly from the cabin.

The early morning air was fresh and mild. The sea and sky were grey, but peaceful. The decks were freshly washed. The sailors in various parts of the ship uncovered their heads. The Colonel and several officers were present. I had earnestly begged to be there also, and finding Mr. George, I stood with my hand in his.

Mrs. Curling's grief had passed the point of tears. She had not shed one since the boy died, though Mrs. Minchin had tried hard to move her to the natural relief of weeping. She only stood in silent agony, though the Quartermaster's cheeks were wet, and most of the ladies sobbed aloud.

As the little coffin slid over the hatchway into the quiet sea, the sun rose, and a long level beam covered the place where the body had gone down.

Then, with a sudden cry, the mother burst into tears.

CHAPTER V.

A HOME STATION—WHAT MRS. BULLER THOUGHT OF IT—WHAT MAJOR BULLER THOUGHT OF IT.

Riflebury, in the south of England—our next station—was a very lively place. "There was always something going on." "Somebody was always dropping in." "People called and stayed to lunch in a friendly way." "One was sure of some one at afternoon tea." "What with croquet and archery in the Gardens, meeting friends on the Esplanade, concerts at the Rooms, shopping, and changing one's novels at the circulating library, one really never had a dull hour." So said "everybody;" and one or two people, including Major Buller, added that "One never had an hour to one's self."

"If you had any one occupation, you'd know how maddening it is," he exclaimed, one day, in a fit of desperation.

"Any one occupation!" cried Mrs. Buller, to whom he had spoken. "I'm sure, Edward, I'm always busy. I never have a quiet moment from morning to night, it seems to me. But it is so like you men! You can stick to one thing all along, and your meals come to you as if they dropped out of the skies, and your clothes come ready-made from the tailor's (and very dearly they have to be paid for, too!); and when one is ordering dinner and luncheon, and keeping one's clothes decent, and looking after the children and the servants, and taking your card, and contriving excuses that are not fibs for you to the people you ought to call on, from week's end to week's end—you say one has no occupation."

"Well, well, my dear," said the Major, "I know you have all the trouble of the household, but I meant to say that if you had any pursuit, any study——"

"And as to visitors," continued Aunt Theresa, who always pursued her own train of ideas, irrespective of replies, "I'm sure society's no pleasure to me; I only call on the people you ought to call on, and keep up a few acquaintances for the children's sake. You wouldn't have us without a friend in the world when the girls come out; and really, what with regimental duties in the morning, and insects afterwards, Edward, you are so absorbed, that if it wasn't for a lady friend coming in now and then, I should hardly have a soul to speak to."

The Major was melted in a moment.

"I am afraid I am a very inattentive husband," he said. "You must forgive me, my dear. And this sprained ankle keeping me in makes me cross, too. And I had so reckoned on these days at home to finish my list of Coleoptera, and get some dissecting and mounting done. But to-day, Mrs. Minchin brought her work directly after breakfast, and that empty-headed fellow Elliott dropped in for lunch, and we had callers all the afternoon, and a *coterie* for tea, and Mrs. St. John (who seems to get through life somehow without the most indefinite notion of how time passes) came in just when tea was over, and you had to order a fresh supply when we should have been dressing for dinner, and the dinner was spoilt by waiting till she discovered that she had no idea (whoever did know her have an idea?) how late it was, and that Mr. St. John would be so angry. And now you want me to go in a cab to a concert at the Rooms to meet all these people over again!"

"I'm sure I don't care for Mrs. St. John a bit more than you do," said Mrs. Buller. "And really she does repeat such things sometimes—without ever looking round to see if the girls are in the room. She told me a thing to-day that old Lady Watford had told her."

"My dear, her ladyship's stories are well known. Cremorne's wife hears them from her, and tells them to her husband, and he tells them to the other fellows. I can always hear them if I wish. But I do not care to. But if you don't like Mrs. St. John, Theresa, what on earth made you ask her to come and sit with you in the morning?"

"Well, my dear, what can I do?" said Mrs. Buller. "She's always saying that everybody is so unsociable, and that she is so dull, she doesn't know what to do with herself, and begging me to take my work and go and sit with her in a morning. How can I go and leave the children and the servants, just at the time of day when everything wants to be set going? So I thought I'd better ask her to come here instead. It's a great bore, but I can keep an eye over the house, and if any one else drops in I can leave them together. It's not me that she wants, it's something to amuse her.

"You talk about my having nothing to do," Aunt Theresa plaintively continued. "But I'm sure I can hardly sleep at night sometimes for thinking of all I ought to do and haven't done. Mrs. Jerrold, you know, made me promise faithfully when we were coming away to write to her every mail, and I never find time. Every week, as it comes round, I think I will, and can't. I used to think that one good thing about coming home would be the no more writing for the English mail; but the Indian mail is quite as bad. And I'm sure mail-day seems to come round quicker than any other day of the week. I quite dread Fridays. And then your mother and sisters are always saying I never write. And I heard from Mrs. Pryce Smith only this morning, telling me I owed her two letters; and I don't know what to say to her when I do write, for she knows nobody *here*, and I know nobody *there*. And we've never returned the Ridgeways' call, my dear. And we've never called on the Mercers since we dined there. And Mrs. Kirkshaw is always begging me to drive out and spend the day at the Abbey. I know she is getting offended, I've put her off so often; and Mrs. Minchin says she is very touchy. And Mrs. Taylor looks quite reproachfully at me because I've not been near the Dorcas meetings for so long. But it's all very well for people who have no children to work at these things. A mother's time is not her own, and charity begins at home. I'm sure I never seem to be at rest, and yet people are never satisfied. Lady Burchett says she's certain I am never at home, for she always misses me when she calls; and Mrs. Graham says I never go out, she's sure, for she never meets me anywhere."

"Isn't all that just what I say?" said Major Buller, laying down his knife and fork. (The discussion took place at dinner.) "It's the tyranny of the idle over the busy; and why, in the name of common sense, should it be yielded to? Why should friends be obliged, at the peril of disparagement of their affection or good manners, to visit each other when they do not want to go—to receive each other when it is not convenient, and to write to each other when there is nothing to say? You women, my dear, I must say, are more foolish in this respect than men. Men simply won't write long letters to their friends when they've nothing to say, and I don't think their friendships suffer by it. And though there are heaps of idle gossiping fellows, as well as ladies with the same qualities, a man who was busy would never tolerate them to his own inconvenience, much less invite them to persecute him. We are more straightforward with each other, and that is, after all, the firmest foundation for friendship. It is partly a misplaced amiability, a phase of the unselfishness in which you excel us, and partly also, I think, a want of some measuring quality that makes you women exact unreasonable things, make impossible promises, and after blandly undertaking a multiplicity of small matters that would tax the method of a man of business to accomplish punctually, put your whole time at the disposal of every fool who is pleased to waste it."

"It's all very well talking, Edward," said Aunt Theresa. "But what is one to do?"

"Make a stand," said the Major. "When you're busy, and can't conveniently see people, let your servant tell them so in as many words. The friendship that can't survive that is hardly worth keeping, I think. Eh, my dear?"

But I suppose the stand was to be made further on, for Major Buller took Aunt Theresa to the concert at "the Rooms."

CHAPTER VI.

DRESS AND MANNER—I EXAMINE MYSELF—MY GREAT-GRANDMOTHER.

When we began our biographies we resolved that neither of us should read the other's till both were finished. This was partly because we thought it would be more satisfactory to be able to go straight through them, partly as a check on a propensity for beginning things and not finishing them, to which we are liable, and partly from the childish habit of "saving up the treat for the last," as we used—in "old times"—to pick the raisins out of the puddings and lay them by for a *bonne bouche* when we should have done our duty by the more solid portion.

But our resolve has given way. We began by very much wishing to break it, and we have ended by finding excellent reasons for doing so.

We both wish to read the biographies—why should we tease ourselves by sticking obstinately to our first opinion?

No doubt it would be nice to read them "straight through." But we are rather apt to devour books at a pace unfavourable to book-digestion, so perhaps it will be better still to read them by bits, as one reads a thing that "comes out in numbers."

And in short, at this point Eleanor took mine, and has read it, and I have read hers. She lays down mine, saying, "But, my dear, you don't remember all this?"

Which is true. What I have recorded of my first English home is more what I know of it from other sources than what I positively remember. And yet I have positive memories of my own about it, too.

I have hinted that my poor young mother did not look after me much. Also that the Ayah, who had a mother's love and care for me, paid very little attention to my being tidy in person or dress, except when I was exhibited to "company."

But my mother was dead. Ayah (after a terrible parting) was left behind in India. And from the time that I passed into Aunt Theresa's charge, matters were quite changed.

I do remember the dresses I had then, and the keen interest I took in the subject of dress at a very early age. A very keen interest was taken in it by Aunt Theresa herself, by Aunt Theresa's daughters, and by the ladies of Aunt

Theresa's acquaintance. I think I may say that it formed (at least one of) the principal subjects of conversation during all those working hours of the day which the ladies so freely sacrificed to each other. Mrs. Buller was truly kind, and I am sure that if I had depended in every way upon her, she would have given to my costume as much care as she bestowed upon that of her own daughters. But my parents had not been poor; there was no lack of money for my maintenance, and thus "no reason," as Aunt Theresa said, why my clothes should not be "decent," and "decent" with Aunt Theresa and her friends was a synonym for "fashionable."

Thus my first black frock was such an improvement (in fashion) upon the pink silk one, as to deprive my deep mourning of much of its gloom. Mrs. (Colonel) St. Quentin could not refuse to lend one of her youngest little girl's frocks as a copy, for "the poor little orphan"; and a bevy of ladies sat in consultation over it, for all Mrs. St. Quentin's things were well worth copying.

"Keep a paper pattern, dear," said Mrs. Minchin; "it will come in for the girls. Her things are always good."

And Mrs. Buller kept a paper pattern.

I remember the dress quite clearly. It is fixed in my mind by an incident connected with it. It had six crape tucks, of which fact I was very proud, having heard a good deal said about it. The first time Mr. George came to our bungalow, after I had begun to wear it, I strutted up to him holding my skirt out, and my head up.

"Look at my black frock, Mr. George," said I; "it has got six crape tucks."

Matilda was most precocious in—at least—one way: she could repeat grown-up observations of wonderful length.

"It's the best crape," she said; "it won't spot. Cut on the bias. They're not real tucks though, Margery. They're laid on; Mrs. Minchin said so."

"They are real tucks," I stoutly asserted.

"No, they're not. They're cut on the bias, and laid on to imitate tucks," Matilda repeated. I think she was not sorry there should be some weak point in the fashionable mourning in which she did not share.

I turned to Mr. George, as usual.

"Aren't they real tucks, Mr. George?"

But Mr. George had a strange look on his face which puzzled and disconcerted me. He only said, "Good heavens!" And all my after efforts were vain to find out what he meant, and why he looked in that strange manner.

Little things that puzzle one in childhood remain long in one's memory. For years I puzzled over that look of Mr. George's, and the remembrance never was a pleasant one. It chilled my enthusiasm for my new dress at the time, and made me feel inclined to cry. I think I have lived to understand it.

But I was not insensible of my great loss, though I took pride in my fashionable mourning. I do not think I much connected the two in my mind. I did not talk about my father to any one but Mr. George, but at night I often lay awake and cried about him. This habit certainly affected my health, and I had become a very thin, weak child when the home voyage came to restore my strength.

By the time we reached Riflebury, my fashionable new dress was neither new nor fashionable. It was then that Mrs. Minchin ferreted out a dressmaker whom Mrs. St. Quentin employed, and I was put under her hands.

The little Bullers' things were "made in the house," after the pattern of mine.

"And one sees the fashion-book, and gets a few hints," said Mrs. Buller.

If Mr. George was not duly impressed by my fashionable mourning, I could (young as I was) trace the effect of Aunt Theresa's care for my appearance on other friends in the regiment. They openly remarked on it, and did not scruple to do so in my hearing. Callers from the neighbourhood patronized me also. Pretty ladies in fashionably pitched bonnets smiled, and said, "One of your little ones, Mrs. Buller? What a pretty little thing!" and duly sympathized over the sad story which Aunt Theresa seemed almost to enjoy relating. Sometimes it was agony to me to hear the oft-repeated tale of my parents' death, and then again I enjoyed a sort of gloomy importance which gave me satisfaction. I even rehearsed such scenes in my mind when I was in bed, shedding real tears as (in the person of Aunt Theresa) I related the sad circumstances of my own grief to an imaginary acquaintance; and then, with dry eyes, prolonging the "fancy" with compliments and consolations of the most flattering nature. I always took care to fancy some circumstances that led to my being in my best dress on the occasion.

Gentleman company did not haunt my new home as was the case with the Indian one. But now and then officers of the regiment called on Mrs. Buller, and would say, "Is that poor Vandaleur's child? Dear me! Very interesting little thing;" and speculate in my hearing on the possibility of my growing up like my mother.

"'Pon my soul, she *is* like her!" said one of the "middle ones" one day, examining me through his eyeglass, "Th' same expressive eyes, you know, and just that graceful gracious little manner poor Mrs. Vandaleur had. By Jove, it was a shocking thing! She was an uncommonly pretty woman."

"You never saw *her* mother, my good fellow," said one of the "old ones" who was present. "She *had* a graceful gracious manner, if you like, and Mrs. Vandaleur was not to be named in the same day with her. Mrs. Vandaleur knew how to dress, I grant you——"

"You may go and play, Margery dear," said Aunt Theresa, with kindly delicacy.

The "old one" had lowered his voice, but still I could hear what he said, as Mrs. Buller saw.

When my father was not spoken of, my feelings were very little hurt. On this occasion my mind was engaged simply with the question whether I did or did not inherit my mother's graces. I ran to a little looking-glass in the nursery and examined my eyes; but when I tried to make them "expressive," I either frowned so unpleasantly, or stared so absurdly, that I could not flatter myself on the point.

The girls were out; I had nothing to do; the nursery was empty. I walked about, shaking out my skirts, and thinking of my gracious and graceful manner. I felt a pardonable curiosity to see this for myself, and, remembering the big glass in Aunt Theresa's room, I stole out to see if I could make use of it unobserved. But the gentlemen had gone, and I feared that Mrs. Buller might come up-stairs. In a few minutes, however, the door-bell rang, and I heard the sound of a visitor being ushered into the drawing-room.

I seized the chance, and ran to Aunt Theresa's room.

The mirror was "full length," and no one could see me better than I now saw myself. Once more I attempted to make expressive eyes, but the result was not favourable to vanity. Then I drew back to the door, and, advancing upon the mirror with mincing steps, I threw all the grace and graciousness of which I was conscious into my manner, and holding out my hand, said, in a "company voice," "*Charmed* to see you, I'm sure!"

"*Mais c'est bien drôle!*" said a soft voice close behind me.

I had not heard the door open, and yet there stood Aunt Theresa on the threshold, and with her a little old lady. The little old lady had a bright, delicately cut face, eyes of whose expressiveness there could be no question, and large grey curls. She wore a large hat, with large bows tied under her chin, and a dark-green satin driving-cloak lined with white and grey fur.

She looked like a fairy godmother, like the ghost of an ancestor—like "somebody out of a picture." She was my great-grandmother.

CHAPTER VII.

MY GREAT-GRANDMOTHER—THE DUCHESS'S CARRIAGE—MRS. O'CONNOR IS CURIOUS.

I was much discomfited. My position was not a dignified one at the best, and in childhood such small shames seem too terrible ever to be outlived. My great-grandmother laughed heartily, and Mrs. Buller, whose sense of humour was small, looked annoyed.

"What in the world are you doing here, Margery?" she said.

I had little or no moral courage, and I had not been trained in high principles. If I could have thought of a plausible lie, I fear I should have told it in my dilemma. As it was, I could not; I only put my hand to my burning cheek, and said:

"Let me see!"

I must certainly have presented a very comical appearance, but the little old lady's smiles died away, and her eyes filled with tears.

"It is strange, is it not," she said to Aunt Theresa, "that, after all, I should laugh at this meeting?"

Then, sitting down on a box by the door, she held out her hands to me, saying:

"Come, little Margery, there is no sin in practising one's good manners before the mirror. Come and kiss me, dear child; I am your father's father's mother. Is not that to be an old woman? I am your great-grandmother."

My great-grandmother's voice was very soft, her cheek was soft, her cloak was soft. I buried my face in the fur, and cried quietly to myself with shame and excitement; she stroking my head, and saying:

"*Pauvre petite!*—thou an orphan, and I doubly childless! It is thus we meet at last to join our hands across the graves of two generations of those we love!"

"It was a dreadful thing!" said Mrs. Buller, rummaging in her pocket for a clean handkerchief. "I'm sure I never should forget it, if I lived a thousand years. I never seemed able to realize that they were gone; it was all so sudden."

The old lady made no answer, and we all wept in silence.

Aunt Theresa was the first to recover herself, and she insisted on our coming down-stairs. A young regimental surgeon and his wife dropped in to lunch, for which my great-grandmother stayed. We were sitting in the drawing-room afterwards, when "Mrs. Vandaleur's carriage" was announced. As my great-grandmother took leave of me, she took off a watch and chain and hung them on my neck. It was a small French watch with an enamelled back of dark blue, on which was the word "Souvenir" in small pearls.

"I gave it to your grandfather long years ago, my child, and he gave it back to me—before he sailed. I would only part with it to his son's child. Farewell, *petite*! Be good, dear child—try to be good. Adieu, Mrs. Buller, and a thousand thanks! Major Buller, I am at your service."

Major Buller took the hand she held out to him and led the old lady to the front door, whither we all followed them.

Mrs. Vandaleur's carriage was before the steps. It was a very quaint little box on two wheels, in by no means good repair. It was drawn by a pony, white, old, and shaggy. At the pony's head stood a small boy in decent, but not smart, plain clothes.

"Put the mat over the wheel to save my dress, Adolphe," said the old lady; and as the little boy obeyed her order she stepped nimbly into the carriage, assisted by the Major. "The silk is old," she observed complacently; "but it is my best, of course, or it would not have been worn to-day," and she gave a graceful little bow towards Aunt Theresa; "and I hope that, with care, it will serve as such for the rest of my life, which cannot be very long."

"If it wears as well as you do, Madam," said Major Buller, tucking her in, "it may; not otherwise."

The Surgeon was leaning over the other side of the little cart, and seemed also to be making polite speeches. It recalled the way that men used to hang upon my mother's carriage. The old lady smiled, and made gracious little replies, and meanwhile deliberately took off her kid gloves, folded, and put them into her pocket. She then drew on a pair of old worsted ones.

"Economy, economy," she said, smiling, and giving a hand on each side of her to the two gentlemen. "May I trouble you for the reins? Many thanks. Farewell, gentlemen! I cannot pretend to fear that my horse will catch cold—his coat is too thick; but you may. Adieu, Mrs. Buller, once more. Farewell, little one, I wish you good-morning, Madam. Adolphe, seat yourself; make your bow, Adolphe. Adieu, dear friends!"

She gave a flick with the whip, which the pony resented by shaking his head; after which he seemed, so to speak, to snatch up the little cart, my great-grandmother, and Adolphe, and to run off with them at a good round pace.

"What an extraordinary turn-out!" said the Surgeon's wife. (She was an Irish attorney's daughter, with the commonest of faces, and the most unprecedented of bonnets. She and her husband had lately "set up" a waggonette, the expense of which just made it difficult for them to live upon their means, and the varnish of which added a care to life.) "Fancy driving down High Street in that!" she continued; "and just when everybody is going out, too!"

"Uncommon sensible little affair, I think," said the Surgeon. "Suits the old lady capitally."

"Mrs. Vandaleur," said Major Buller, "can afford to be independent of appearances to an extent that would not perhaps be safe for most of us."

"You're right there, Buller," said the Surgeon. "Wonderfully queenly she is! That fur cloak looks like an ermine robe on her."

"I don't think you'd like to see me in it!" tittered his wife.

"I don't say I should," returned the Surgeon, rather smartly.

"My dear," said Mrs. Buller, "you must make up your mind to be jealous of the Duchess. All gentlemen are mad about her."

"The Duchess!" said Mrs. O'Connor, in a tone of respect. "I thought you said——"

"Oh, she is not really a duchess, my dear; it's only a nickname. I'll tell you all about it some day. It's a long story."

Discovering that Mrs. Vandaleur was a family connection, and not a chance visitor from the neighbourhood, Mrs. O'Connor apologized for her remarks, and tried to extract the Duchess's history from Aunt Theresa then and there. But Mrs. Buller would only promise to tell it "another time."

"I'm dying with curiosity," said Mrs. O'Connor, as she took leave, "I shall run in to-morrow afternoon on purpose to hear all about it. Can you do with me, dear Mrs. Buller?"

"Pray come," said Aunt Theresa warmly, with an amiable disregard of two engagements and some arrears of domestic business.

I was in the drawing-room next day when Mrs. O'Connor arrived.

"May I come in, dear Mrs. Buller?" she said, "I won't stay two minutes; but I *must* hear about the Duchess. Now, *are* you busy?"

"Not at all," said Aunt Theresa, who was in the midst of making up her tradesmen's books. "Pray sit down, and take off your bonnet."

"It's hardly worth while, for I *can't* stay," said Mrs. O'Connor, taking her bonnet off, and setting it down so as not to crush the flowers.

As Mrs. O'Connor stayed two hours and a half, and as Aunt Theresa granted my request to be allowed to hear her narrative, I learnt a good deal of the history of my great-grandmother.

CHAPTER VIII.

A FAMILY HISTORY.

"We are not really connected," Mrs. Buller began. "She is Margery's great-grandmother, and Margery and I are second cousins. That's all. But I knew her long ago, before my poor cousin Alice married Captain Vandaleur. And I have heard the whole story over and over again."

I have heard the story more than once also. I listened with open mouth to Aunt Theresa at this time, and often afterwards questioned her about my "ancestors," as I may almost call them.

Years later I used to repeat these histories to girls I was with. When we were on good terms they were interested to hear, as I was proud to tell, and would say, "Tell us about your ancestors, Margery." And if we fell out there was no surer method of annoying me than to slight the memory of my great-great-grandparents.

I have told their story pretty often. I shall put it down here in my own way, for Aunt Theresa told a story rather disconnectedly.

The de Vandaleurs (we have dropped the *de* now) were an old French family. There was a Duke in it who was killed in the Revolution of '92, and most of the family emigrated, and were very poor. The title was restored afterwards, and some of the property. It went to a cousin of the Duke who was murdered, he having no surviving children; but they say it went in the wrong line. The cousin who had remained in France, and always managed to keep the favour of the ruling powers, got the title, and remade his fortunes; the others remained in England, very poor and very proud. They would not have accepted any favours from the new royal family, but still they considered themselves deprived of their rights. One of these Vandaleur *émigrés* (the one who ought to have been the Duke) had married his cousin. They suffered great hardships in their escape, I fancy, and on the birth of their son, shortly after their arrival in England, the wife died.

There was an old woman, Aunt Theresa said, who used to be her nurse when she was a child, in London, who had lived, as a girl, in the wretched lodgings where these poor people were when they came over, and she used to tell her wonderful stories about them. How, in her delirium (she was insane for some little time before her son was born), Madame de Vandaleur fancied herself in her old home, "with all her finery about her," as Nurse Brown used to say.

Nurse Brown seems to have had very little sympathy with nervous diseases. She could understand a broken leg, or a fever, "when folks kept their beds"; but the disordered fancies of a brain tried just too far, the mad whims of a lady who could "go about," and who insisted upon going about, and changing her dress two or three times a day, and receiving imaginary visitors, and ordering her faithful nurse up and down under the names of half-a-dozen servants she no longer possessed, were beyond her comprehension.

Aunt Theresa said that she and her brothers and sisters had the deepest pity for the poor lady. They thought it so romantic that she should cry for fresh flowers and dress herself to meet the Queen in a dirty little lodging at the back of Leicester Square, and they were always begging to hear "what else she did." But Nurse Brown seems to have been fondest of relating the smart speeches in which she endeavoured to "put sense into" the devoted French servant who toiled to humour every whim of her unhappy mistress, instead of being "sharp with her," as Nurse Brown advised. Aunt Theresa had some doubts whether Mrs. Brown ever did make the speeches she reported; but when people say they said this or that, they often only mean that this or that is what they wish they had said.

"If she's mad, I says, shave her head, instead of dressing her hair all day long. I've knowed mad people as foamed at the mouth and rolled their eyes, and would have done themselves a injury but for a strait-jacket; and I've knowed folks in fevers unreasonable enough, but they kept their beds in a dark room, and didn't know their own mothers. Madame's ways is beyond me, I says. *You* calls it madness: *I* calls it temper. Tem—per, and no—thing else."

Aunt Theresa used to make us laugh by repeating Nurse Brown's sayings, and the little shake of herself with which she emphasized the last sentence.

If she had no sympathy for Madame de Vandaleur, she had a double share for the poor lady's husband: "a *good* soul," as she used to call him. It was in vain that Jeanette spoke of the sweet temper and unselfishness of her mistress "before these terrible days"; her conduct towards her husband then was "enough for" Nurse Brown, so she said. No sooner had the poor gentleman gone off on some errand for her pleasure than she called for him to be with her, and was only to be pacified by a fable of Jeanette's devising, who always said that "the King" had summoned Monsieur de Vandaleur. Jeanette was well aware that, the childless old Duke being dead, her master had succeeded to the title, and she often spoke of him as Monsieur le Duc to his wife, which seems to have pleased the poor lady. When he was absent, Jeanette's ready excuse, "*Eh, Madame! Pour Monsieur le Duc—le Roi l'a fait appeller,*" was enough, and she waited patiently for his return.

Ever-changing as her whims and fancies were, the poor gentleman sacrificed everything to gratify them. His watch, his rings, his buckles, the lace from his shirt, and all the few trifles secured in their hasty flight, were sold one by one. His face was familiar to the keepers of certain stalls near to where Covent Garden Market now stands. He bought flowers for Madame when he could not afford himself food. He sold his waistcoat, and buttoned his coat across him—and looked thinner than ever.

Then the day came when Madame wished, and he could not gratify her wish. Everything was gone. He said, "This will kill me, Jeanette;" and Jeanette believed him.

Nurse Brown (according to her own account) assured Jeanette that it would not. "Folk doesn't die of such things, says I."

But, in spite of common-sense and experience, Monsieur de Vandaleur did die of grief, or something very like it, within twenty-four hours of the death of his wife, and the birth of their only son.

For some years the faithful Jeanette supported this child by her own industry. She was an exquisite laundress, and she throve where the Duke and Duchess would have starved. As the boy grew up she kept him as far as possible from common companions, treated him with as much deference as if he had succeeded to the family honours, and filled his head with traditions of the deserts and dignity of the de Vandaleurs.

At last a cousin of Monsieur de Vandaleur found them out. He also was an exile, but he had prospered better, had got a small civil appointment, and had married a Scotch lady. It was after he had come to the help of his young kinsman, I think, that an old French lady took a fancy to the boy, and sent him to school in France at her own expense. He was just nineteen when she died, and left him what little money she possessed. He then returned to England, and paid his respects to his cousin and the Scotch Mrs. Vandaleur.

She congratulated herself, I have heard, that her only child, a daughter, was from home when this visit was paid.

Mrs. Janet Vandaleur was a high-minded, hard-headed, north-country woman. She valued long descent, and noble blood, and loyalty to a fallen dynasty like a Scotchwoman, but, like a Scotchwoman, she also respected capability and energy and endurance. She combined a romantic heart with a practical head in a way peculiar to her nation. She knew the pedigree of every family (who had a pedigree) north of the Tweed, and was, probably, the best housekeeper in Great Britain. She devoutly believed her own husband to be as perfect as mortal man may be here below, whilst in some separate compartment of her brain she had the keenest sense of the defects and weaknesses which he inherited, and dreaded nothing more than to see her daughter mated with one of the helpless Vandaleurs.

This daughter, with much of her mother's strong will and practical capacity, had got her father's *physique* and a good deal of his artistic temperament. Dreading the development of *de Vandaleur* qualities in her, the mother made her education studiously practical and orderly. She had, like most Scotch matrons of her type, too good a gift for telling family stories, and too high a respect for ancestral traditions, to have quite kept herself from amusing her daughter's childhood with tales of the de Vandaleur greatness. But after her husband discovered his young relative, and as their daughter grew up, she purposely avoided the subject, which had, probably, the sole effect of increasing her daughter's interest in the family romance. Mrs. Janet knew the de Vandaleur pedigree as well as her own, and had shown a miniature of the late Duke in his youth to her daughter as a child on many occasions; when she had also alluded to the fact that the title by birth was undoubtedly in the exiled branch of the family. Miss Vandaleur was not ignorant that the young gentleman who had just completed his education was, if every one had their rights, Monsieur le Duc; and she was as much disappointed to have missed seeing him as her mother was glad that they had not met.

For Bertrand de Vandaleur had all the virtues and the weaknesses of his family in intense proportions. He had a hopeless ignorance of the value of money, which was his strongest condemnation before his Scotch cousin. He was high-minded, chivalrous, in some points accomplished, charming, and tender-hearted. But he was weak of will, merely passive in endurance, and quite without energy. He had a graceful, fanciful, but almost weak intellect. I mean, it just bordered on mental deficiency; and at times his dreamy eyes took a wildness that was said to make him painfully like his mother in her last days. He was an absurd but gracefully romantic idea of his family consequence. He was very handsome, and very like the miniature of the late Duke. It was most desirable that his cousin should not meet him, especially as she was of the sentimental age of seventeen. So Mrs. Janet Vandaleur hastened their return from London to their small property in Scotland.

But there was no law to hinder Monsieur de Vandaleur from making a Scotch tour.

One summer's afternoon, when she had just finished the making of some preserves, Miss Vandaleur strolled down through a little wood behind the house towards a favourite beck that ran in a gorge below. She was singing an old French song in praise of the beauty of a fair lady of the de Vandaleurs of olden time. As she finished the first verse, a voice from a short distance took up the refrain—

"Victoire de Vandaleur! Victoire! Victoire!"

It was her own name as well as that of her ancestress, and she blushed as her eyes met those of a strange young gentleman, with a sketch-book in his hand, and a French poodle at his heels.

"Place aux dames!" said the stranger. On which the white poodle sat up, and his master bowed till his head nearly touched the ground.

They had met once as children, which was introduction enough in the circumstances. Here, at last, for Victoire, was the embodiment of all her dreams of the de Vandaleur race. He was personally so like the miniature, that he might have been the old Duke. He was the young one, as even her mother allowed. For him, he found a companion whose birth did not jar on his aristocratic prejudices, and whose strong character was bone and marrow to his weak one. Before they reached the house Mrs. Janet's precautions were vain.

She grew fond of the lad in spite of herself. The romantic side of her sympathized with his history. He was an orphan, and she had a mother's heart. In the direct line he was a Duke, and she was a Scotchwoman. He freely consented to settle every penny he had upon his wife, and, as his mother-in-law justly remarked, "Many a cannier man wouldn't just have done that."

In fine, the young people were married with not more than the usual difficulties beforehand.

He was nineteen, and she was seventeen. They were my great-grandfather and great-grandmother.

They had only one child—a son. They were very poor, and yet they gave him a good education. I ought to say, *she* gave him, for everything that needed effort or energy was done by my great-grandmother. The more it became evident that her Bertrand de Vandaleur was less helpful and practical than any Bertrand de Vandaleur before him, the more there seems to have developed in her the purpose and capability inherited from Mrs. Janet. Like many another poor and ambitious mother, she studied Latin and Greek and algebra that she might teach her son. And at the same time she saved, even out of their small income. She began to "put by" from the boy's birth for his education, and when the time came he was sent to school.

My grandfather did well. I have heard that he inherited his father's beauty, and was not without his mother's sense and energy. He had the de

Vandaleur quality of pleasing, with the weakness of being utterly ruled by the woman he loved. At twenty he married an heiress. His parents had themselves married too early to have reasonable ground for complaint at this; but when he left his own Church for that of his wife, there came a terrible breach between them and their only son. His mother soon forgave him; but the father was as immovable in his displeasure as weak people can sometimes be. Happily, however, after the birth of a grandson peace was made, and the young husband brought his wife to visit his parents. The heiress had some property in the West Indies, which they proposed to visit, and they remained with the old people till just before they sailed. It was as a keepsake at parting that my grandfather had restored to his mother the watch which she gave to me. The child was left in England with his mother's relations.

My grandfather and grandmother never returned. They were among the countless victims of the most cruel of all seas. The vessel they went out in was lost during a week of storms. On what day or night, and in what part of the Atlantic, no one survived to tell.

Their orphan child was my dear father.

CHAPTER IX.

HOPES AND EXPECTATIONS—DREAMS AND DAY DREAMS—THE VINE—ELSPETH—MY GREAT-GRANDFATHER.

My father was brought up chiefly by his mother's relations. The religious question was always a difficulty as regarded the de Vandaleurs, and I fancy extended to my own case. My guardians were not my great-grandparents, but Major Buller, and Mr. Arkwright, a clergyman of the Church of England. My great-grandfather and great-grandmother were Roman Catholics. Though not my appointed guardians, they were my nearest relations, and when my great-grandmother had held out her little hand towards me over the side of the pony-carriage and said, "You will let the child come to me? Soon, very soon?" Major Buller had taken her hand in both his, and replied very cordially, "Of course, my dear madam, of course. Whenever it is convenient to yourself and to Mr. de Vandaleur."

And this promise had stirred my heart with such a flutter of happy expectation as I had not felt since I persuaded my father to promise that I should dine with him, all alone, like a grown-up lady, on that sad birthday on which he died.

It is perhaps useless to try and find reasons for the fancy I took to the "Duchess"—as Aunt Theresa called her—since it was allowed that she fascinated every one who came near her. With the bright qualities which made her admirable in herself, she combined the gracious art of putting other people at ease with themselves; and, remembering how sore the wounds of a child's self-love are, I think that her kindness must have been very skilful to make me forgive myself for that folly of the looking-glass enough to forget myself in admiration of her.

Like most children, I was given to hero and heroine worship. I admired more than one lady of Aunt Theresa's acquaintance, and had been fascinated by some others whom I did not know, but had only seen in church, and had longed for the time when I also should no longer trip about in short and simple skirts, and tie up my curls with a ribbon, but should sweep grandly and languidly in to the parade service, bury half a pew under the festoons and furbelows of my silk dress and velvet trimmings, sink into a nest ofmatchless millinery for the Litany, scent the air with patchouli as I rose for the hymn, examine the other ladies' bonnets through one of those eyeglasses which are supposed to make it no longer rude to stare, and fan myself from the fatigues of the service during the sermon.

But even the dignity of grown-updom embellished by pretty faces and splendid costumes did not stir my imagination as it was stirred by the sight of my great-grandmother and by the history of her life. It was like seeing the princess of a fairy tale with one's very own eyes. The faces of the fine ladies I had envied were a little apt to be insipid in expression, and to pass from the memory; but my great-grandmother's quick, bright, earnest face was not easily to be forgotten. I made up my mind that when I grew up I would not wear a large *chignon* after all, nor a bonnet full of flowers, nor a dress full of flounces, but a rather short skirt and buckled shoes and grey curls, and a big hat with many bows, and a green satin driving-cloak lined with fur.

How any one, blessed with grown-up freedom of choice, could submit to be driven about by a coach-man in a big carriage, as highly stuffed and uninteresting as a first-class railway carriage, when it was possible to drive one's self in a sort of toy-cart with a dear white pony as shaggy as a dog, I could not understand. I well knew which I should choose, and I thought so much of it that I remember dreaming that my great-grandmother had presented me with a pony and chaise the counterpart of her own. The dream-joy of this acquisition, and the pride of driving up to the Bullers' door and offering to take Matilda for an expedition, was only marred by one of those freaks which spoil the pleasure of so many dreams. Just as Matilda appeared, full of gratitude, and with a picnic luncheon in a basket, I became conscious that I was in my night-gown, and had forgotten to dress. Again and again I tried to go back in my dream and put on suitable clothes. I never accomplished it, and only woke in the effort.

In sober daylight I indulged no hope that Mrs. Vandaleur would give me a carriage and pony for my very own, but I did hope that I should go out in hers if ever I went to stay with her. Perhaps sometimes alone, driving myself, with only the rosy-cheeked Adolphe to open the gates and deliver me from any unexpected difficulties with the reins. But I dreamed many a day-dream of the possible delights in store for me with my new-found relatives, and almost counted the hours on the Duchess's watch till she should send for me.

As it happened, however, circumstances combined for some little time to hinder me from visiting my great-grandmother.

The little Bullers and I had the measles; and when we were all convalescent, Major Buller got two months' leave, and we went away for change of air. Then small-pox prevailed in Riflebury, and we were kept away, even after Major Buller returned to his duties. When we did return, before a visit to the Vandaleurs could be arranged, Adolphe fell ill of scarlet fever, and the fear of contagion postponed my visit for some time.

I was eight years old when I went to stay at The Vine. This was the name of the little cottage where my great-grandparents lived—so called because of an old vine which covered the south wall on one side of the porch, and crept over a framework upon the roof. I do not now remember how many pounds of grapes it had been known to produce in one season, and yet I ought not to have forgotten, for it was a subject on which my great-grandfather, my great-grandmother, Adolphe, and Elspeth constantly boasted.

"And if they don't just ripen as the master says they do in France, it's all for the best," said Elspeth; "for ripe grapes would be picked all along, and the house not a penny the better for them. But green-grape tarts and cream are just eating for a king."

Elspeth was "general servant" at my great-grandmother's. Her aunt Mary had come from Scotland to serve "Miss Victoire" when she first married. As Mary's health failed, and she grew old, her young niece was sent for to work under her. Old Mary died with her hands in my great-grandmother's, and Elspeth reigned in her stead.

Elspeth was an elderly woman when I first made her acquaintance. She had a broad, bright, sensible face, and a kindly smile that won me to her. She wore frilled caps, tied under her chin; and as to exchanging them for "the fly-away bits of things servants stick on their heads at the present time," Elspeth would as soon have thought of abandoning the faith of her fathers. She was a strict but not bitter Presbyterian. She was not tall, and she was very broad; her apparent width being increased by the very broad linen collars which spread, almost like a cape, over her ample shoulders.

My great-grandmother had an anecdote of me connected with this, which she was fond of relating.

"And what do you think of Elspeth, little one?" she had said to me on the first evening of my visit.

"I think she's very big," was my reply.

"Certainly, our good Elspeth is as wide as she is tall," said my great-grandfather, laughing.

I wondered if this were so; and when my great-grandmother gave me a little yard-measure in a wooden castle, which had taken my fancy among the treasures of her work-box, the idea seized me of measuring Elspeth for my own satisfaction on the point. But the silken measure slipped, and caught on the battlements of the castle, and I lost my place in counting the figures, and at last was fain to ask Elspeth herself.

"How tall are you, Elspeth, please? As much as a yard?"

"Ou aye, my dear," said Elspeth, who was deeply engaged in darning a very large hole in one of my great-grandfather's socks.

"As much as two yards?" I inquired.

"Eh, no, my dearie," said Elspeth. "That wad be six feet; and I'm not just that tall, though my father was six feet and six inches."

"How broad are you, Elspeth, please?" I persisted. "As much as a yard?"

"I'm thinking I will be, my dear," said Elspeth, "for it takes the full width of a coloured cotton to cut me a dress-front, and then it's not over-big."

"Are you as broad as two yards, do you think?" I said, drawing my ribbon to its full length from the castle, and considering the question.

Elspeth shook her head. She was biting the end off a piece of darning-cotton; but I rightly concluded that she would not confess to being two yards wide.

"Please, I have measured Elspeth," I announced over the tea-table, "and grandpapa is quite right."

"Eh?" said Mr. Vandaleur, who had a trick of requiring observations to be repeated to him by his wife.

"She says that she has measured Elspeth, and that you are right," said my great-grandmother. "But about what is grandpapa right, my little one?"

"Grandpapa said that Elspeth is as wide as she is tall," I explained. "And so she is, for I measured her—at least, the ribbon would slip when I measured her, so I asked her; and she's a yard tall, but not as much as two yards; and a yard wide, but not as much as two yards. And so grandpapa is right."

Some of the happiest hours I spent at The Vine were spent in Elspeth's company. I made tiny cakes, and tarts of curious shapes, when she was busy pastry-making, and did some clear-starching on my doll's account when Elspeth was "getting-up" my great-grandfather's cravats.

Elspeth had strong old-fashioned notions of paying respect where it was due. She gave Adolphe a sharp lecture one day for some lack of respect in his manner to "Miss Margery"; and, on the other hand, she taught me to curtsy at the door where I breakfasted with Mr. and Mrs. Vandaleur.

Some dancing lessons that I had had in Riflebury helped me here, and Elspeth was well satisfied with my performance. I felt very shy and awkward the first time that I made my morning curtsy, my knees shaking under me, and Elspeth watching from the passage; but my great-grandfather and mother seemed to take it as a matter of course, and I soon became quite used to it. If

Mr. Vandaleur happened to be standing in the room, he always returned my curtsy by a low bow.

I became very fond of my great-grandfather. He was a tall, handsome old man, with high shoulders, slightly bent by age and also by habit. He wore a blue coat with brass buttons, that had been very well made a very long time ago; white trousers, a light waistcoat, a frilled shirt, and a very stiff cravat. On the wall of the drawing-room there hung a water-colour portrait of a very young and very handsome man, with longish wavy hair, features refined to weakness, dreamy, languid eyes, and a coat the very image of my great-grandfather's. The picture hung near the door; and as Mr. Bertrand Vandaleur passed in or out, I well remember that he almost always glanced at the sketch, as people glance at themselves in passing a mirror.

I was too young then to notice this as being a proof that the drawing was a portrait of himself; but I remember being much struck by the likeness between the coat in the picture and that my great-grandfather wore, and also by the way that the hair was thrown back from the high, narrow forehead, just as my great-grandfather's grey hairs were combed away from his brow. Children are great admirers of beauty too, especially, I think, of an effeminate style of good looks, and are very susceptible to the power of expression in faces. I had a romantic admiration for "the handsome man by the door," and his eyes haunted me about the room.

I was kneeling on a chair and examining the sketch one morning, when my great-grandfather came up to me, "Who is it, little one?" said he.

I looked at the picture. I looked at my great-grandfather's coat. As his eyes gazed steadily into mine, there was a likeness there also; but it was the coat that decided me. I said, "It is you, grandpapa."

I think this little incident just sealed our friendship. I always remained in high favour with my great-grandfather.

He spent a great deal of his time in painting. He never had, I believe, had any profession. The very small income on which he and his wife had lived was their own private fortune. I often think it must have been a great trial to a woman of my great-grandmother's energy, that her husband should have made no effort to add to their resources by work of some kind. But then I cannot think of any profession that would have suited him. He was sadly wanting in general capacity, though accomplished much above the average, and with a fine knack in the budding of roses.

I thought him the grandest gentleman that ever lived, and the pleasantest of companions. His weak but lovable nature had strong sympathy with children, I think. I ought to say, with a child; for he would share the fancies and humours of one child companion for hours, but was quite incapable of managing a larger number—as, indeed, he was of any kind of domestic administration or control. Mrs. Vandaleur was emphatically Elspeth's mistress, if she was also her friend; but in the absence of "the mistress" Elspeth ruled "the master" with a rod of iron.

I quickly gained a degree of power over him myself. I discovered that if I maintained certain outward forms of respect and courtesy, so as not to shock my grandpapa's standard of good manners, I might make almost any demands on his patience and good-nature. Children and pet animals make such discoveries very quickly, and are apt to use their power somewhat tyrannically. I fear I was no exception to the rule.

CHAPTER X.

THOMAS THE CAT—MY GREAT-GRANDFATHER'S SKETCHES—ADOLPHE IS MY FRIEND—MY GREAT-GREAT-GREAT-GRANDFATHER DISTURBS MY REST—I LEAVE THE VINE.

My great-grandfather had, as I said, some skill in painting. He was gifted with an intense sense of, and love for, colour. I am sure he saw colours where other people did not. What to common eyes was a mass of grey, or green, was to him a pleasant combination of many gay and delicate hues. He distinguished severally the innumerable bright threads in Nature's coat of many colours, and in simple truth I think that each was a separate joy to him.

He had a white Persian cat of an artistic temperament, which followed him in his walks, dozed on the back of his arm-chair, and condescended to share his tea when it reached a certain moderate temperature. It never was betrayed into excitement, except when there was fish for dinner. My great-grandfather's fasts were feasts for Thomas the cat.

I can very clearly remember the sight of my great-grandfather pacing slowly up and down the tiny garden at The Vine, his hands behind him, and followed sedately by Thomas. Now and then he would stop to gaze, with infinite contentment in his eyes, at the delicate blue-grey mist behind the leafless trees (which in that spring sunshine were, no doubt, of much more complex and beautiful colour to him than mere brown), or drinking in the blue of the scillas in the border with a sigh of satisfaction. When he paused, Thomas would pause; as he feasted his eyes, Thomas would rub his head against his master's legs, and stretch his own. When Elspeth had cooked the fish, and my great-grandmother had made the tea and arranged the flowers on the table, they would come in together and condescend to their breakfasts, with the same air about them both of having no responsibility in life but to find out sunny spots and to enjoy themselves.

My great-grandfather's most charming paintings were sketches of flowers. Ordinary stiff flower-paintings are of all paintings the most uninteresting, I think; but his were of a very different kind. Each sketch was a sort of idyll. Indeed, he would tell me stories of each as he showed them.

Long as my great-grandfather had lived, he was never a robust man, and Elspeth's chief ideas on the subject of his sketches bore reference to the colds he had caught, and the illnesses he had induced, by sitting in the east winds or lying on damp grass to do this or that sketch.

"That'll be the one the master did before he was laid by with the rheumatics," Elspeth said, when I described one of my favourites to her. It was a spring sketch. My great-grandfather had lain face downwards on the lawn to do it. This was to bring his eyes on a level with the subject of his painting, which was this: a crocus of the exquisite shades of lilac to be seen in some varieties, just full-blown, standing up in its first beauty and freshness from its fringe of narrow silver-striped leaves. The portrait was not an opaque and polished-looking painting on smooth cardboard, but a sketch—indefinite at the outer edges of the whole subject—on water-colour paper of moderate roughness. The throat and part of the cup of the flower stood out from some shadow at the roots of a plant beyond; a shadow of infinite gradation, and quite without the blackness common to patches of shade as seen by untrained eyes. From the level of my great-grandfather's view, as he lay in the grass, the border looked a mere strip; close behind it was a hedge dividing the garden from a field. Just by the crocus there was a gap in the hedge, which in the sketch was indicated rather than drawn. And round the corner of the bare thorn branches from the hedge-bank in the field there peeped a celandine and a daisy. They were not nearly such finished portraits as that of the crocus. A few telling strokes of colour made them, and gave them a life and pertness that were clever enough. Beneath the sketch was written, "La Demoiselle. Des enfants du village la regardent."

My great-grandfather translated this for me, and used to show me how the "little peasants," Marguerite and Celandine, were peeping in at the pretty young lady in her mauve dress striped with violet.

But every sketch had its story, and often its moral; not, as a rule, a very original one. In one, a lovely study of ivy crept over a rotten branch upon the ground. A crimson toadstool relieved the heavy green, and suggested that the year was drawing to a close. Beneath it was written, "Charity." "Thus," said my great-grandfather, "one covers up and hides the defects of one he loves."

A study of gaudy summer tulips stood—as may be guessed—for Pride.

"Pride," said my great-grandfather, "is a sin; a mortal sin, dear child. Moreover, it is foolish, and also vulgar—the pride of fine clothes, money, equipages, and the like. What is called pride of birth—the dignity of an ancient name—this, indeed, is another thing. It is not petty, not personal; it seems to me more like patriotism—the pride of country."

I did my best to describe to Elspeth both the sketch and my great-grandfather's commentary.

"A' pride's sinful," said Elspeth decidedly. "Pride o' wealth, and pride o' birth. Not that I'm for objecting to a decent satisfaction in a body's ain gude conduct and respectability. Pride o' character, that's anither thing a'thegither, and to be respectit."

My great-grandfather gave me a few paints, and under his directions I daubed away, much to my own content. When I was struggling hopelessly with the perspective of some pansies of various colours (for in imitation of him I painted flowers), he would say, "Never mind the shape, dear Marguerite, get the colour—the colour, my child!" And he trained me to a quickness in the perception of colour certainly not common at my age.

I spent many pleasant hours, too, in the less intellectual society of Adolphe. He dug a bed for me in a bit of spare ground, and shaped it like a heart. He laboured constantly at this heart, making it plump by piling up the earth, and cramming it with plants of various kinds—perennials much in want of subdivision, and often in full bloom—which he brought from cottage gardens of "folk he knew," and watered copiously to "sattle 'em."

His real name was not Adolphe, but Thomas. As this, however, had created some confusion between him and the cat, my great-grandmother had named him afresh, after a retainer of the de Vandaleurs in days gone by, whose faithful service was a tradition in the family.

I was very happy at The Vine—by day. I feel ashamed now to recall how miserable I was at night, and yet I know I could not help it. In old times I had always been accustomed to be watched to sleep by Ayah. After I came to Aunt Theresa, I slept in the same room with one or more of the other children. At The Vine, for the first time, I slept alone.

This was not all. It was not merely the being alone in the dark which frightened me. Indeed, a curious little wick floating on a cup of oil was lighted at night for my benefit, but it only illumined the great source of the terror which made night hideous to me.

Some French refugee artist, who had been indebted to my great-grandparents for kindness, had shown his gratitude by painting a picture of the execution of that Duc de Vandaleur who perished in the Revolution, my great-grandfather having been the model. It was a wretched daub, but the subject was none the less horrible for that, and the caricatured likeness to my great-grandfather did not make it seem less real or more pleasant.

That execution which was never over, this ghastly head which never found rest in the grave, that awful-looking man who was, and yet was not, Grandpapa—haunted me. They were the cause of certain horrible dreams, which I can remember quite as clearly at this day as if I dreamed them last night, and which I know I shall never forget. The dreams again associated themselves with the picture, and my fears grew instead of lessening as the time went by.

Very late one night Elspeth came in and found me awake, and probably looking far from happy. I had nothing to say for myself, but I burst into tears. Elspeth was tenderness itself, but she got hold of a wrong idea. I was "just homesick," she thought, and needed to be "away home again," with "bairns like myself."

I do not know why I never explained the real reason of my distress—children are apt to be reticent on such occasions. I think a panic seized upon the members of the household, that they were too old to make a child happy. I was constantly assured that "it was very natural," and I "had been very good." But I was sent back to Riflebury. No one knew how loth I was to leave, still less that it was to a much older relative than those at The Vine that I owed my expulsion—to my great-great-great-grandfather—Monsieur le Duc de Vandaleur.

Thomas, the cat, purred so loudly as I withdrew, that I think he was glad to be rid of me.

Adolphe alone was against the verdict of the household, and I think believed that I would have preferred to remain.

"I'm sure I thought you was quite sattled, miss," he said, as he saw me off; and he blubbered like a baby. His transplanted perennials were "sattled" by copious floods of water. Perhaps he hoped that tears would settle me!

CHAPTER XI.

MATILDA'S NEWS—OUR GOVERNESS—MAJOR BULLER TURNED TUTOR—ELEANOR ARKWRIGHT.

The grief I felt at leaving The Vine was greatly forgotten in the warm welcome which awaited me on my return to Riflebury.

In a household where gossip is a principal amusement, the return of any member from a visit is a matter for general congratulation till the new budget is exhausted. Indeed, I plead guilty to a liking to be the first to skim the news when Eleanor or one of the boys comes back from a visit, at the present time.

Matilda withdrew me from Aunt Theresa as soon as she could.

"I am so glad to get you back, Margery dear," said she. "And now you must tell me all your news, and I'll tell you all mine. And to begin with—what do you think?—we've got a governess, and you and I are to have the little room at the head of the stairs all to ourselves."

Matilda's news was lengthy enough and interesting enough to make us late for tea, and mine kept us awake for a couple of hours after we were fairly in our two little iron bedsteads in the room that was now our very own. That is to say, I told what I had to tell after we came to bed, but my news was so tame compared with Matilda's that we soon returned to the discussion of hers. I tried to describe my great-grandfather's sketches, but neither Aunt Theresa in the drawing-room, nor Matilda when we retired for the night, seemed to feel any interest in the subject; and when Mrs. Buller asked what sort of people called at The Vine, I felt that my reply was, like the rest of my news, but dull.

Matilda's, on the contrary, was very entertaining. She spoke enthusiastically of Miss Perry, the governess.

"She is so good-natured, Margery, you can't think. When lessons are over she takes me walks on the Esplanade, and she calls me her dear Matilda, and I take her arm, and she tells me all about herself. She says she knows she's very romantic. And she's got lots of secrets, and she's told me several already; for she says she has a feeling that I can keep a secret, and so I can. But telling you's not telling, you know, because she's sure to tell you herself; only you'd better wait till she does before you say anything, for fear she should be vexed."

Of course I promised to do so, and craned my neck out of bed to catch Matilda's interesting but whispered revelations.

Matilda herself was only partially in Miss Perry's confidence, and I looked anxiously forward to the time when she would admit me also to her secrets, though I feared she might consider me too young. My fears were groundless, as I found Miss Perry was fond of talking about herself, and a suitable audience was quite a secondary consideration with her.

She was a *protégée* of Mrs. Minchin's, who had persuaded Aunt Theresa to take her for our governess. She was quite unfit for the position, and did no little harm to us in her brief reign. But I do not think that our interests had entered in the least into Mrs. Minchin's calculations in the matter. She had "taken Miss Perry up," and to get Miss Perry a comfortable home was her sole object.

To do our new governess justice, she did her best to impart her own superficial acquirements to us. We plodded regularly through French exercises, which she corrected by a key, and she kept us at work for a given number of hours during the day; tatting by our sides as we practised our scales, or roasting her petticoats over the fire, whilst Matilda and I read Mrs. Markham's *England* or Mrs. Trimmer's *Bible Lessons* aloud by turns to full-stops. But when lessons were over Miss Perry was quite as glad as we were, and the subjects of our studies had as little to do with our holiday hours as a Sunday sermon with the rest of the week.

She was a great novel-reader, and I think a good many of the things she told us of, as having happened to herself, had their real origin in the Riflebury circulating library. For she was one of those strange characters who indulge in egotism and exaggeration, till they seem positively to lose the sense of what is fact and what is fiction.

She filled our poor empty little heads with a great deal of folly, and it was well for us that her reign was not a long one.

She was much attached to the school-room fireside. She could not sit too close to it, or roast herself too thoroughly for her own satisfaction. I sometimes wondered if the bony woman who kept the library ever complained of the curled condition of the backs of the books Miss Perry held between her eyes and the hot coals for so many hours.

In this highly heated state our governess was, of course, sensitive to the smallest inlet of cooler air, and "draughts" were accordingly her abhorrence. How we contrived to distinguish a verb from a noun, or committed anything whatever to memory in the fever-heat and "stuffy" atmosphere of the little room which was sacred to our studies, I do not know. At a certain degree of the thermometer Miss Perry's face rises before me and makes my brain spin even now.

This was, no doubt, one cause of the very severe headaches to which Matilda became subject about this time, though, now I look back, I do not think she had been quite strong since we all had the measles. They were apt to end in a fainting condition, from which she recovered by lying on the floor. Then, if Miss Perry happened to be in good humour, she would excuse Matilda from further lessons, invariably adding, in her "mystery" voice —"But not a word to your mamma!"

It was the most unjustifiable use she made of influence she gained over us (especially over poor Matilda, who was very fond of her, and believed in her) that she magnified her own favours at the expense of Major Buller and my aunt. For some time they had no doubts as to the wisdom of Mrs. Minchin's choice.

Miss Perry was clever enough not to display her romantic side to Mrs. Buller. She amused her, too, with Riflebury gossip, in which she was an adept. She knew equally well how far she might venture with the Major; and the sleight-of-hand with which she threw needlework over a novel when Aunt Theresa came into the school-room was not more skilful than the way in which she turned the tail of a bit of scandal into a remark upon the weather as Uncle Buller opened the drawing-room door.

But Miss Perry was not skilful enough to win the Major's lasting favour. He was always slow to interfere in domestic matters, but he was not unobservant.

"I'm sure you see a great deal more than one would think, Edward," Aunt Theresa would say; "although you are so wrapt up in insects and things."

"The insects don't get into my eyes, my dear," said Major Buller.

"And hear too," Mrs. Buller continued. "Mrs. O'Connor was saying only the other day that you often seem to hear of things before other people, though you do talk so little."

"It is, perhaps, because I am not always talking that I do hear. But Mrs. O'Connor is not likely to think of that," said the Major, rather severely.

He was neither blind nor deaf in reference to Miss Perry, and she was dismissed. Aunt Theresa rather dreaded Mrs. Minchin's indignation in the matter, I believe; but needlessly, for Miss Perry and Mrs. Minchin quarrelled about this time, and Mrs. Minchin had then so much information to Miss Perry's disadvantage at her fingers' ends, that it seemed wonderful that she should ever have recommended her.

For some little time our education progressed in a very desultory fashion.

Major Buller became perversely prejudiced against governesses, and for a short time undertook to carry on our English lessons himself. He made sums amusing, and geography lessons "as good as stories," though the latter so often led (by very interesting channels) to his dearly beloved insects, that Mrs. Buller accused him of making our lessons an excuse for getting out his "collection."

With "grammar" we were less successful. Major Buller was so good a teacher that he brought out what intelligence we possessed, and led us constantly to ask questions about anything we failed to understand. In arithmetic this led to his helping us over our difficulties; in geography it led, sooner or later, to the "collection"; but in English grammar it led to stumbling-blocks and confusion, and, finally, to the Major's throwing the book across the room, and refusing to pursue that part of our education any further.

"I never learnt English grammar," said the Major, "and it's quite evident that I can't teach it."

"If *you* don't know grammar, Papa, then *we* needn't," said Matilda promptly, and being neat of disposition, she picked up the book and proceeded to put it away.

"I never said that I didn't know grammar," said the Major; "I fancy I can speak and write grammatically, but what I know I got from the Latin grammar. And, upon my soul," added Uncle Buller, pulling at his heavy moustache, "I don't know why you shouldn't do the same."

The idea of learning Latin pleased us greatly, and Major Buller (who had been at Charterhouse in his boyhood) bought a copy of Dr. Russell's *Grammar*, and we set to work. And either because the rules of the Latin grammar bore explanation better than the English ones, or because Major Buller was better able to explain them, we had no further difficulties.

We were very proud of doing lessons in these circumstances, and boasted of our Latin, I remember, to the little St. Quentins, when we met them at the dancing-class. The St. Quentins were slender, ladylike girls, much alike, and rendered more so by an exact similarity of costume. Their governess was a very charming and talented woman, and when Mrs. St. Quentin proposed that Matilda and I should share her daughters' French lessons under Miss Airlie, Major Buller and Aunt Theresa thankfully accepted the offer. I think that our short association with this excellent lady went far to cure us of the silly fancies and tricks of vulgar gossip which we had gleaned from Miss Perry.

So matters went on for some months, much to Matilda's and my satisfaction, when a letter from my other guardian changed our plans once more.

Mr. Arkwright's only daughter was going to school. He wrote to ask the Bullers to let her break the journey by spending a night at their house. It was a long journey, for she was coming from the north.

"They live in Yorkshire," said Major Buller, much as one might speak of living in Central Africa.

Matilda and I looked forward with great interest to Miss Arkwright's arrival. Her name, we learnt, was Eleanor, and she was nearly a year older than Maria.

"She'll be *your* friend, I suppose," I said, a little enviously, in reference to her age.

"Of course," said Matilda, with dignity. "But you can be with us a good deal," she was kind enough to add.

I remember quite well how disappointed I felt that I should have so little title to share the newcomer's friendship.

"If she had only been ten years old, and so come between us," I thought, "she would have been as much mine as Matilda's."

I little thought then what manner of friends we were to be in spite of the five years' difference in age. Indeed, both Matilda and I were destined to see more of her than we expected. Aunt Theresa and Major Buller came to a sudden resolution to send us also to the school where she was going, though we did not hear of this at first.

Long afterwards, when we were together, Eleanor asked me if I could remember my first impression of her. For our affection's sake I wish it had been a picturesque one; but truth obliges me to confess that, when our visitor did at last arrive, Matilda and I were chiefly struck by the fact that she wore thick boots, and did not wear crinoline.

And yet, looking back, I have a very clear picture of her in my mind, standing in the passage by her box (a very rough one, very strongly corded, and addressed in the clearest of handwriting), purse in hand, and paying the cabman with perfect self-possession. An upright, quite ladylike, but rather old-fashioned little figure, somewhat quaint from the simplicity of her dress. She had a rather quaint face, too, with a nose slightly turned up, a prominent forehead, a charming mouth, and most beautiful dark eyes. Her hair was rolled under and tied at the top of her head, and it had an odd tendency to go astray about the parting.

This was, perhaps, partly from a trick she seemed to have of doing her hair away from the looking-glass. She stood to do it, and also (on one leg) to put on her shoes and stockings, which amused us. But she was always on her feet, and seemed unhappy if she sat idle. We took her for a walk the morning after her arrival, and walked faster than we had ever walked before to keep pace with our new friend, who strode along in her thick boots and undistended skirts with a step like that of a kilted Highlander.

When we came into the town, however, she was quite willing to pause before the shop-windows, which gave her much entertainment.

"I'm afraid I should always be looking in at the windows if I lived in a town," she said, "there are such pretty things."

Eleanor laughs when I remind her of that walk, and how we stood still by every chemist's door because she liked the smell. When anything interested her, she stopped, but at other times she walked as if she were on the road to some given place, and determined to be there in good time; or perhaps it would be more just to say that she walked as if walking were a pleasure to her. It was walking—not strolling. When she was out alone, I know that she constantly ran when other people would have walked. It is a north-country habit, I think. I have seen middle-aged Scotch and Yorkshire ladies run as lightly as children.

It was not the fashionable time of day, so that we could not, during that walk, show Eleanor the chief characters of Riflebury. But just as we were leaving High Street she stopped and asked, "Who is that lady?"

"The one in the mauve silk?" said Matilda. "That is one of the cavalry ladies. All the cavalry ladies dress grandly."

It was a Mrs. Perowne. She was sailing languidly down the other side of the street, in a very large crinoline, and a very long dress of pale silk, which floated after her along the dirty pavement, much, I remember, to my admiration. Above this was some tight-fitting thing with a good deal of lace about it, which was crowned by a fragile and flowery bonnet, and such a tuft of white lace at the end of a white stick as just sheltered her nose, which was aquiline, from the sunshine. She was prettily dressed for an open carriage, a flower-show, or a wedding breakfast; for walking through the streets of a small, dirty town, to change her own books at the library, her costume was ludicrously out of place, though at the time I thought it enviably grand. The way in which a rich skirt that would not wash, and would undoubtedly be worn again, trailed through dust and orange-peel, and greengrocers' refuse, and general shop-sweepings, was offensive to cleanliness alone.

"Is she ill?" Eleanor asked.

"No," said Matilda; "I don't think so. Why?"

"She walks so slowly," said Eleanor, gazing anxiously at Mrs. Perowne out of her dark eyes, "and she is so white in the face."

"Oh, my dear!" said Matilda, laughing, "that's puff—puff, and a white veil. It's to make her look young. I heard Mrs. Minchin tell Mamma that she knew she was thirty-seven at least. But she dresses splendidly. If you stay over Sunday, you'll see her close, for she sits in front of us in church. And she has such a splendid big scent-bottle, with gold tops, and such a lovely, tiny little prayer-book, bound in blue velvet, and a watch no bigger than a shilling, with a monogram on the back. She took it out several times in the sermon last Sunday, so I saw it. But isn't her hair funny?"

"It's a beautiful colour," said Eleanor, "only it looks different in front. But I suppose that's the veil."

"No, it isn't," said Matilda; "that's the new colour for hair, you know. It's done by stuff you put on; but Miss Perry said the worst was, it didn't always come out the same all over. Lots of ladies use it."

"How horrid!" said Eleanor. "But what makes her walk so slow?"

"Well, I don't know," said Matilda. "Why should she walk quick?"

Eleanor seemed struck by this reply, and after a few minutes' pause, said very gently, with a slight blush on her cheeks, "I'm afraid I have been walking too fast for you. I'm used to walking with boys."

We earnestly assured her that this was not the case, and that it was much better fun to walk with her than with Miss Perry, who used to dawdle so that we were often thoroughly chilled.

In the afternoon we took her to the Esplanade, when Matilda, from her knowledge of the people, took the lead in the conversation. I was proud to walk on the other side of our new friend, with my best doll in my arms. Aunt Theresa came with us, but she soon sat down to chat to a friend, and we three strolled up and down together. I remember a pretty bit of trimming on Eleanor's hat being blown by the wind against her face, on which she quietly seized it, and stuffed it securely into the band.

"Oh, my dear!" said Matilda, in the emphatic tone in which Aunt Theresa's lady visitors were wont to exclaim about nothing in particular —"don't do that. It looks so pretty; and you're crushing it *dreadfully*."

"It got in my eyes," said Eleanor briefly. "I hate tags."

We went home before Aunt Theresa, but as we stood near the door, Eleanor lingered and looked wistfully up the road, which ran over a slight hill towards the open country.

"Would you like to stay out a little longer?" we politely asked.

"I should rather like to go to the top of the hill," said Eleanor. "Don't you think flat ground tires one? Shall we race up?" she added.

We willingly agreed. I had a few yards start of Eleanor, and Matilda rather less, and away we went. But we were little used to running, and hoops and thin boots were not in our favour. Eleanor beat us, of course. She seemed in no way struck by the view from the top. Indeed it was not particularly pretty.

"It's very flat about here," she said. "There are no big hills you can get to the top of, I suppose?"

We confessed that there were not, and, there being nothing more to do, we ran down again, and went indoors.

Eleanor dressed for the evening in her usual peripatetic way, and, armed with a homely-looking piece of grey knitting, followed us down-stairs.

Her superabundant energy did not seem to find vent in conversation. We were confidential enough now to tell each other of our homes, and she had sat so long demurely silent, that Matilda ventured upon the inquiry—

"Don't you talk much at your home?"

"Oh yes," said Eleanor—"at least, when we've anything to say;" and I am sure no irony was intended in the reply.

"What are you knitting, my dear?" said Aunt Theresa.

"A pair of socks for my brother Jack," was the answer.

"I'm sure you're dreadfully industrious," said Mrs. Buller.

A little later she begged Eleanor to put it away.

"You'll tire your eyes, my dear, I'm sure; pray rest a little and chat to us."

"I don't look at my knitting," said Eleanor; but she put it away, and then sat looking rather red in the face, and somewhat encumbered with her empty hands, which were red too.

I think Uncle Buller noticed this; for he told us to get the big scrap-book and show it to Miss Arkwright.

Eleanor got cool again over the book; but she said little till, pausing before a small, black-looking print in a sheet full of rather coarse coloured caricatures, cuttings from illustrated papers and old-fashioned books, second-rate lithographs, and third-rate original sketches, fitted into a close patchwork, she gave a sort of half-repressed cry.

"My dear! What is it?" cried Matilda effusively.

"I think," said Eleanor, looking for information to Aunt Theresa, "I think it's a real Rembrandt, isn't it?"

"A real what, my dear?" said Mrs. Buller.

"One of Rembrandt's etchings," said Eleanor; "and of course I don't know, but I think it must be an original; it's so beautifully done, and my mother has a copy of this one. We know ours is a copy, and I think this must be an original, because all the things are turned the other way; and it's very old, and it's beautifully done," Eleanor repeated, with her face over the little black print.

Major Buller came across the room, and sat down by her.

"You are fond of drawing?" he said.

"Very," said Eleanor, and she threw a good deal of eloquence into the one word.

The Major and she forthwith plunged into a discussion of drawing, etching, line-engraving, &c., &c. It appeared that Mrs. Arkwright etched on copper, and had a good collection of old etchings, with which Eleanor was familiar. It also transpired that she was a naturalist, which led by easy stages to a promise from the Major to show Eleanor his insects.

They talked till bedtime, and when Aunt Theresa bade us good-night, she said:

"I'm glad you've found your voice, my dear;" and she added, laughing, "But whenever Papa talks to anybody, it always ends in the collection."

CHAPTER XII.

POOR MATILDA—THE AWKWARD AGE—MRS. BULLER TAKES COUNSEL WITH HER FRIENDS—THE "MILLINER AND MANTUAMAKER"—MEDICAL ADVICE—THE MAJOR DECIDES.

It was not because Major Buller's high opinion of Miss Airlie was in any way lowered that he decided to send us to school. In fact it was only under long and heavy pressure, from circumstances as well as from Aunt Theresa, that he gave his consent to a plan which never quite met with his approval.

Several things at this time seemed to conspire to effect it. The St. Quentins were going on long leave, and Miss Airlie would go with them. This was a heavy blow. Then we heard of this school after Miss Airlie had left Riflebury, a fact so opportune as to be (so Aunt Theresa said) "quite providential." If we were to go to school, sending us to this one would save the trouble of making personal inquiries, and perhaps a less wise selection, for Major Buller had confidence in Mr. Arkwright's good judgment. The ladies to whose care his daughter was confided were probably fit to teach us.

"It would save a great deal of trouble," my guardian confessed, and it must also be confessed that Major Buller was glad to avoid trouble when he could conscientiously do so.

I think it was his warm approval of Eleanor which finally clinched the question. He thought that she would be a good companion for poor Matilda.

Why I speak of her as "poor Matilda" demands some explanation.

Before I attempt to give it I must say that there is one respect in which our biographies must always be less satisfactory than a story that one might invent. When you are putting down true things about yourself and your friends, you cannot divide people neatly into the good and the bad, the injurers and the injured, as you can if you are writing a tale out of your head. The story seems more complete when you are able either to lay the blame of the melancholy events on the shoulders of some unworthy character, or to show that they were the natural punishment of the sufferer's own misconduct. But in thinking of Matilda and Aunt Theresa and Major Buller, or even of the Doctor and Mrs. Buller's lady friends, this is not possible.

The morbid condition—of body and mind—into which Matilda fell for some time was no light misfortune either as regards her sufferings or the discomfort it produced in the household, and I am afraid she was both mismanaged and in fault herself.

It is safe, at any rate, to take the blame for one's own share, and I have often thought, with bitterness of spirit, that, child as I was, I might have been both forbearing and helpful to Matilda at a time when her temper was very much tried by ill-health and untoward circumstances. We had a good many squabbles about this period. I piqued myself upon generally being in the right, and I did not think then, as I do now, that it is possible to be most in the right in a quarrel, and at the same time not least to blame for it.

Matilda certainly did by degrees become very irritable, moody, and perverse, and her perversity developed itself in ways which puzzled poor Aunt Theresa.

She became silent and unsociable. She displayed a particular dislike to the privileges of being in the drawing-room with grown-up "company," and of accompanying Aunt Theresa when she paid her afternoon calls. She looked very ill, and stoutly denied that she was so. She highly resented solicitude on the subject of her health, fought obstinately over every bottle of medicine, and was positively rude to the doctors.

For her unsociability, I think, Miss Perry's evil influence was partly to blame. Poor Matilda clung to her belief in our late governess when she was no more to us than a text upon which Aunt Theresa and her friends preached to each other against governesses in general, and the governesses each had suffered from in particular. Our lessons with Major Buller, and the influence of Miss Airlie's good breeding and straightforward kindness, gave a healthier turn to our tastes; but when Miss Airlie went away and Major Buller proclaimed a three weeks' holiday from the Latin grammar, and we were left to ourselves, Matilda felt the want of the flattery, the patronage, and the small excitements and mysteries about nothing, to which Miss Perry had accustomed her. I blush to think that my companionship was less comfort to her than it ought to have been. As to Aunt Theresa, she was always too busy to give full attention to anything; and this does not invite confidence.

Another reason, I am sure, for Matilda's dislike to appearing in company was a painful sense of her personal appearance; and as she had heard Aunt Theresa and her friends discuss, approve, and condemn their friends by the standard of appearances alone, ever since she was old enough to overhear company conversation, I hardly think she was much to blame on this point.

Matilda was emphatically at what is called "an awkward age"; an age more awkward with some girls than with others. I wish grown-up ladies, who mean to be kind to their friends' daughters, would try to remember the awkwardness of it, and not increase a naturally uncomfortable self-consciousness by personal remarks which might disturb the composure of older, prettier, and better-dressed people. It is bad enough to be quite well aware that the size of one's hands and feet prematurely foreshadow the future growth of one's figure; that these are the more prominent because the simple dresses of the unintroduced young lady seem to be perpetually receding from one's bony-wrists above, and shrinking towards the calves of one's legs below, from those thin ankles on which one is impelled to stand by turns (like a sleeping stork) through some mysterious instinct of relieving the weak and overgrown spine.

This, I say, is mortifying enough, and if modesty and good breeding carry us cheerfully through a not unfelt contrast with the assured manners and flowing draperies of Mamma's lady friends in the drawing-room, they might spare us the announcement of what it hardly needs gold eyeglasses to discover—that we really grow every day. Blushes come heavily enough to hands and cheeks when to the shyness of youth are added the glows and chills of imperfect circulation: it does not need the stare of strangers, nor the apologies of Mamma, to stain our doubtful complexions with a deeper red.

All girls are not awkward at the awkward age. I speak most disinterestedly on Matilda's behalf, for I never went through this phase myself. It is perhaps because I am small that I can never remember my hands, or any other part of me, feeling in my way; and my clothes—of whatever length, breadth, or fashion—always had a happy knack of becoming one with me in such wise that I could comfortably forget them.

The St. Quentin girls were nearer to Matilda's age than I, but they too were very happy and looked very nice in the hobble-de-hoy stage of girlhood. I am sure that they much preferred the company of their young brothers to the company of the drawing-room; but they did what they were told to do, and seemed happy in doing it. They had, however, several advantages over Matilda. By judicious care (for they were not naturally robust) they were kept in good health. They kept a great many pets, and they always seemed to have plenty to do, which perhaps kept them from worrying about themselves. Adelaide, for instance, did all the flowers for the drawing-room and dinner-table. Mrs. St. Quentin said she could not do them so well herself. They had a very small garden to pick from, but Adelaide used lots of wild-flowers and grass and ferns. She often let me help her to fill the china jars, and she was the only person who ever seemed to like hearing about Grandpapa's paintings. They all did something in the house. But I believe that their greatest advantage over poor Matilda was that they had not been accustomed to hear dress and appearance talked about as matters of the first importance, so that whatever defects they felt conscious of in either did not weigh too heavily on their minds.

On poor Matilda's they weighed heavily indeed. And she was not only troubled by that consciousness of being plain, by which I think quite as many girls are affected as by the vanity of being pretty (and which has received far less attention from moralists); she was also tormented by certain purely nervous fancies of her face being swollen, her eyes squinting, and her throat choking, when people looked at her, which were due to ill-health.

Unhappily, the ill-health which was a good excuse for Matilda's unwillingness to "play pretty" in the drawing-room was the subject on which she was more perverse than any other. It was a great pity that she was not frank and confiding with her mother. The detestable trick of small concealments which Miss Perry had taught us was partly answerable for this; but the fault was not entirely Matilda's.

Aunt Theresa had not time to attend to her. What attention she did give, however, made her so anxious on the subject that she took counsel with every lady of her acquaintance, and the more she talked about poor Matilda's condition the less leisure she had to think about it.

"It may be more mind than body, I'm afraid," said Aunt Theresa one afternoon, on our return from some visiting in which Matilda had refused to share. "Mrs. Minchin says she knew a girl who went out of her senses when she was only two years older than Matilda, and it began with her refusing to go anywhere or see any one."

Major Buller turned round on his chair with an anxious face, and a beetle transfixed by a needle in his hand.

"It was a very shocking thing," continued Aunt Theresa, taking off her bonnet; "for she had a great-uncle in Hanwell, and her grandfather cut his throat. I suppose it was in the family."

Major Buller turned back again, and pinned the beetle by its proper label.

"I suppose it was," said he dryly; "but as there is no insanity in my family or in yours that I'm aware of, Mrs. Minchin's case is not much to the point."

"Mrs. O'Connor won't believe she's ill," sighed Aunt Theresa; "*she* thinks it's all temper. She says her own temper was unbearable till she had it knocked out of her at school."

"Matilda's temper was good enough till lately," growled the Major.

"She says Dr. O'Connor's brother, who is the medical officer of a lunatic asylum somewhere in Tipperary," continued Aunt Theresa, "declares all mad women go out of their minds through ill-temper. He's written a book about it."

"Heaven defend me, mind and body, from the theories of that astute practitioner!" said Uncle Buller piously.

"It's all very well making fun of it, but everybody tells one that girls are more trouble than any number of boys. I'm sure I don't remember giving my mother any particular trouble when I was Matilda's age, but the stories I've heard to-day are enough to make one's hair stand on end. Mrs. Minchin knew another girl, who lost all her appetite just like Matilda, and she had a very sulky temper too, and at last they found out she used to eat black-beetles. She was a Creole, or something of that sort, I believe, but they couldn't stop her. The Minchins knew her when they were in the West Indies, when he was in the 209th; or, at least, it was there they heard about her. The houses swarmed with black-beetles."

"A most useful young lady," said Uncle Buller. "Does Matilda dine on our native beetles, my dear? She hasn't touched my humble collection."

"Oh, if you make fun of everything——" Aunt Theresa began; but at this moment Mrs. St. John was announced.

After the customary civilities, Aunt Theresa soon began to talk of poor Matilda, and Mrs. St. John entered warmly into the subject.

To do the ladies of the regiment justice, they sympathized freely with each other's domestic troubles; and indeed it was not for lack of taking counsel that any of them had any domestic troubles at all.

"Girls are a good deal more difficult to manage than boys, I'm afraid," sighed Aunt Theresa, repeating Mrs. O'Connor's *dictum.*

"Women are *dreadful* creatures at any age," said Mrs. St. John to the Major, opening her brown eyes in the way she always does when she is talking to a gentleman. "I always *longed* to have been a man."

[Eleanor says she hates to hear girls say they wish they were boys. If they do wish it, I do not myself see why they should not say so. But one thing has always struck me as very odd. If you meet a woman who is incomparably silly, who does not know an art or a trade by which she could keep herself from starvation, who could not manage the account-books of a village shop, who is unpunctual, unreasoning, and in every respect uneducated—a woman, in short, who has, one would think, daily reason to be thankful that her necessities are supplied by other people, she is pretty sure to be always regretting that she is not a man.

Another, trick that some silly ladies have *riles* me (as we say in Yorkshire) far more than this odd ambition for responsibilities one is quite incompetent to assume. Mrs. St. John had it, and as it was generally displayed for the benefit of gentlemen, who seem as a rule to be very susceptible to flattery, I suppose it is more a kind of drawing-room "pretty talk" than the expression of deliberate opinions. It consists of contrasting girls with boys and women with men, to the disparagement of the former, especially in matters over which circumstances and natural disposition are commonly supposed to give them some advantage.

I remember hearing a fat, good-natured girl at one of Aunt Theresa's garden-parties say, with all the impressiveness of full conviction, "Girls are far more cruel than boys, really. You know, women are *much* more cruel than men—oh, I'm *sure* they are!" and the idea filled me not less with amazement than with horror. This very young lady had been most good-natured to us. She had the reputation of being an unselfish and much-beloved elder sister. I do not think she would have hurt a fly. Why she said this I cannot imagine, unless it was to please the young gentleman she was talking to. I think he did look rather gratified. For my own part, the idea worried my little head for a long time—children give much more heed to general propositions of this kind than is commonly supposed.]

There was one disadvantage in the very fulness of the sympathy the ladies gave each other over their little affairs. The main point was apt to be neglected for branches of the subject. If Mrs. Minchin consulted Mrs. Buller about a cook, that particular cook might be discussed for five minutes, but the rest of a two hours' visit would probably be devoted to recollections of Aunt Theresa's cooks past and present, Mrs. Minchin's "coloured cooks" in Jamaica, and the cooks engaged by the mothers and grandmothers of both ladies.

Thus when Aunt Theresa took counsel with her friends about poor Matilda, they hardly kept to Matilda's case long enough even to master the facts, and on this particular occasion Mrs. St. John plunged at once into a series of illustrative anecdotes of the most terrible kind, for she always talked, as she dressed, in extremes. The moral of every story was that Matilda should be sent to school.

"And I'll send you over last year's numbers of the *Milliner and Mantua-maker*, dear Mrs. Buller. There are always lots of interesting letters about people's husbands and children, and education, and that sort of thing, in the column next to the pastry and cooling drinks receipts. There was a wonderfully clever letter from a 'M.R.C.S.' about the difficulty of managing young girls, and recommending a strict school where he had sent his daughter. And next month there were long letters from five 'British Mothers' and 'A Countess' who had not been able to manage their daughters, and had sent them to this school, and were in every way satisfied. Mr. St. John declared that all the letters were written by one person to advertise the school, but he always does say those sort of things about anything I'm interested in."

"You're very kind," said Mrs. Buller.

"There was a most extraordinary correspondence, too, after that shoemaker's daughter in Lambeth was tried for poisoning her little brother," continued Mrs. St. John. "The *Saturday Review* had an article on it, I believe, only Mr. St. John can't bring papers home from the mess, so I didn't see it. The letters were all about all the dreadful things done by girls in their teens. There were letters from twelve 'Materfamiliases,' I know, because the editor had to put numbers to them, and four 'Paterfamiliases,' and 'An Anxious Widower,' and 'A Minister,' and three 'M.D.'s.' But the most awful letter was from 'A Student of Human Nature,' and it ended up that every girl of fifteen was a murderess at heart. If I can only lay my hand on that number—— but I've lent it to so many people, and there was a capital paper pattern in it too, of the *jupon à l'Impératrice*, ready pricked."

At this point Uncle Buller literally exploded from the room. Aunt Theresa said something about draughts, but I think even Mrs. St. John must have been aware that it was the Major who banged the door.

I was sitting on the footstool by the fire-place making a night-dress for my doll. My work had been suspended by horror at Mrs. St. John's revelations, and Major Buller's exit gave an additional shock in which I lost my favourite needle, a dear little stumpy one, with a very fine point and a very big eye, easy to thread, and delightful to use.

When Mrs. St. John went away Major Buller came back.

"I am sorry I banged the door, my dear," said he kindly, "but whatever the tempers of girls may be made of at fifteen, mine is by no means perfect, I regret to say, at fifty; and I *cannot* stand that woman. My dear Theresa, let me implore you to put all this trash out of your head and get proper medical advice for the child at once. And—I don't like to seem unreasonable, my dear, but—if you must read those delectable articles to which Mrs. St. John refers, I wish you'd read them at her house, and not bring them into ours. I'd rather the coarsest novel that ever was written were picked up by the children, if the broad lines of good and evil were clearly marked in it, than this morbid muddle of disease and crime, and unprincipled parents and practitioners."

Uncle Buller seldom interfered so warmly; indeed, he seldom interfered at all. I think Aunt Theresa would have been glad if he would have advised her oftener.

"Indeed, Edward," said she, "I'll do anything you think right. And I'm sure I wouldn't read anything improper myself, much less let the children. And as to the *Milliner and Mantuamaker* you need not be afraid of that coming into the house unless I send for it. Mrs. St. John is always promising to lend me the fashion-book, but she never remembers it."

"And you'll have proper advice for Matilda at once?"

"Certainly, my dear."

Mrs. Buller was in the habit of asking the regimental Surgeon's advice in small matters, and of employing a civilian doctor (whose fees made him feel better worth having) in serious illness. She estimated the seriousness of a case by danger rather than delicacy. So the Surgeon came to see Matilda, and having heard her cough, promised to send a "little something," and she was ordered to keep indoors and out of draughts, and take a tablespoonful three times a day.

Matilda had not gone graciously through the ordeal of facing the principal Surgeon in his uniform, and putting out her tongue for his inspection; and his prescriptions did not tend to reconcile her to being "doctored." Fresh air was the only thing that hitherto had seemed to have any effect on her aches and pains, or to soothe her hysterical irritability, and of this she was now deprived. When Aunt Theresa called in an elderly civilian practitioner, she was so sulky and uncommunicative, and so resolutely refused to acknowledge to any ailments, that (his other prescriptions having failed to cure her lassitude, and his pompous manner and professional visits rather provoking her feverish perversity) the old doctor also recommended that she should be sent to school.

Medical advice is very authoritative, and yet Uncle Buller hesitated.

"It's like packing a troublesome son off to the Colonies, my dear," said he. "And though Dr. Brown may be justified in transferring his responsibilities elsewhere, I don't think that parents should get rid of theirs in this easy fashion."

But when Eleanor came, the Major's views underwent a change. If I went with Matilda, and we had Eleanor Arkwright for a friend, he allowed that he would consent.

"That is if the girl is willing to go. I will send no child of mine out of my house against her will."

Major Buller asked her himself. Asked with so much kindness, and expressed such cheery hopes that change of air, regular occupation, and the society of other young people would make her feel "stronger and happier" than she had seemed to be of late, that to say that Matilda would have gone anywhere and done anything her father wished is to give a feeble idea of the gush of gratitude which his sensible and sympathetic words awoke in her. Unfortunately she could not keep herself from crying just when she most wanted to speak, and Uncle Buller, having a horror of "scenes," cut short the one interview in which Matilda felt disposed to confide in her parents.

But she confided to me, when she came to bed that night (*I* didn't mind her crying between the sentences), that she was very, very sorry to have been "so cross and stupid," and that if we were not going to school she meant to try and be very different. I begged her to let me ask Uncle Buller to keep us at home a little longer, but Matilda would not hear of it.

"No, no," she sobbed, "not now. I should like to do something he and Mamma want, and they want us to go to school."

For my own part I was quite willing to go, especially after I had seen Eleanor Arkwright. So we were sent—to Bush House.

CHAPTER XIII.

AT SCHOOL—THE LILAC-BUSH—BRIDGET'S POSIES—SUMMER—HEALTH.

We knew when it was summer at Bush House, because there was a lilac-tree by the gate, which had one large bunch of flowers on it in the summer when Eleanor and I and Matilda were at school there. As we left the house in double file to take our daily exercise on the high-road, the girls would bob their heads to catch a whiff of the scent as they passed, or to let the cool fragrant flowers brush their foreheads. On this point Madame, our French governess, remonstrated in vain. We took turns for the side next to the lilac, and sniffed away as long as there was anything to smell. Even when the delicate colour began to turn brown, and the fragrance vanished, we were loth to believe that the blossoms were fading.

"I think I have got a cold in my head," said Matilda, who had plunged her nose into the cluster one day in vain.

"You have a cough, ma foi! Mademoiselle Buller," replied Madame, who seemed to labour under the idea that Matilda rather enjoyed this privilege. But I had tried the lilac-bush myself with no better success.

"I think," I whispered to Eleanor, in English, "that we have smelt it all up."

"Parlez-vous français, mesdemoiselles!" cried Madame, and we filed out into the dusty street, at the corner of which sat another of our visible tokens of the coming of the season of flowers; a dirty, shrivelled old Irishwoman, full of benedictions and beggary, who, all through the summer, sold "posies" to the passers-by. We school-girls were good customers to her. We were all more or less sentimental, more or less homesick, and had more or less of that susceptibility to the influence of scents which may, some day, be the basis of a new school of medicine. One girl had cultivated pinks and *Roses de Meaux* in her own garden "at home," and Bridget was soon wise enough to discover that a nosegay composed of these materials was an irresistible temptation to that particular customer. Another had a craving for the sight and smell of southernwood (or "old man," as Eleanor called it), and preferred it in combination with bachelor's buttons.

"There was an old woman 'at home' whom we used to go to tea with when we were children—my brother and I," she said; "there were such big bunches of southernwood by her cottage. And bachelor's buttons all round the garden."

The brother was dead, I knew, and there were two flattened "buttons" and a bit of withered "old man" gummed into her Bible. "Picked the last day we were out together. Before he was taken ill with scarlet fever," she told me. She had the boy's portrait in a standing frame, and, little space as we had in our bedrooms, the other girls piled their brushes and ribbon-boxes on one side of the looking-glass as best they could, and left the rest of the dressing-table sacred to his picture, and to the Bible, and the jar of Bridget's flowers, which stood before the likeness as if it had been that of a patron saint.

For my own part I was very ignorant of the names and properties of English flowers. I knew some by sight, from Adelaide St. Quentin's bouquets, and from my great-grandfather's sketches; and I knew the names of others of which Adolphe had given me plants, and of which I was glad to see the flower. As I had plenty of pocket-money I was a liberal customer, and I made old Bridget tell me the names of the flowers in her bunches. I have since found out that whenever she was at fault she composed a name upon the spot, with the ready wit and desire to please characteristic of her nation. These names were chiefly connected with the Blessed Virgin and the saints.

"The Lord blesh ye, my dear," she would say; "that's 'Mary's flower';" or, "Sure it's the 'Blessed Virgin's spinning-wheel,' and a pretty name too!"

A bitter-smelling herb which she commended to me as "Saints' Savory," I afterwards learned to be tansy.

The youngest of us, a small, silent little orphan, had bought no posy till one day she quietly observed, "If you could get me a peony, I would buy it."

The peony was procured; so large, so round, and so red, that some one unfeelingly suggested that it should be cut up for pickled cabbage. The little miss walked home with it in her hand, looking at it as sentimentally as if it had been a forget-me-not. As we had been hard-hearted enough to laugh at it, we never learned the history which made it dear.

Madame would certainly never have allowed us to break our ranks, and chaffer with Bridget, but that some one had been lucky enough to think of giving her bouquets.

Madame liked flowers—as ornaments—and was sentimental herself, after a fashion, a sentimentality of appearances. She liked a bright spot of colour on her sombre dresses too, and she was economical; for every day that she had a bright bouquet a day's wear and tear was saved to her neck-ribbons. She pinned the bright flowers by her very clean collar, and not very clean throat, and permitted us to supply ourselves also from Bridget's basket.

A less pleasant sign of summer than the lilac-blossom or Bridget's flower-basket was the heat. It was hot in the dusty, draughty streets of the little town. The empty bedrooms at Bush House were like ovens, and the well-filled school-room was much worse. Madame would never hear any complaints of the heat from me or from Matilda. Summer at Bush House, in the nature of things, could be nothing to summer in India, to which we were accustomed. It was useless to point out that in India the rooms in which we lived were large, well shaded, and ventilated by constant currents of fresh air. Also that there, our heaviest meal, our longest walk, and our hardest work were not all crowded into the hottest hours of the day.

"England is at no time so warm as India," said Madame.

"I suppose we are not as hot as the cook," suggested little "Peony" as we now called her, one very hot day, when we sat languidly struggling through our work in the stifling atmosphere of the school-room. "I thought of her to-day when I looked at that great fat leg of roast mutton. We're better off than she is."

"And she's better off than if she were in the Black Hole of Calcutta; but that doesn't make either her or us cool," said Emma Lascelles, an elder girl. "Don't preach, Peony; lessons are bad enough in this heat."

"I shan't eat any dinner to-morrow, I think," said Eleanor; "I cannot keep awake after it this weather, so it's no use."

"I wish I were back at Miss Martin's for the summer," said another girl.

We knew to what this referred, and Madame being by a rare chance absent, we pressed for an account, in English, of Miss Martin's arrangements in the hot weather. "Miss Martin's" was a school at which this girl had been before she came to Bush House.

"I can't think why on earth you left her," said Eleanor.

"Well, this is nearer home for one thing, and the masters are better here, certainly. But she did take such care of us. It wasn't everlasting backaches, and headaches, and coughs, and pains in your side all along. And when the weather got hot (and it was a very warm summer when I was there), and she found we got sleepy at work after dinner, and had headaches in the afternoon, she said she thought we had better have a scrap meal in the middle of the day, and dine in the cool of the evening; and so we used to have cold rice-pudding or thick bread-and-butter, such as we should have had for tea, or anything there was, and tumblers of water, at one, and at half-past five we used to wash and dress; and then at six, just when we were getting done up with the heat and work, and yet cool enough to eat, we had dinner. I can tell you a good fat roast leg of mutton looked all right then! It cured all our headaches, and we worked twice as well, both at midday work and at getting lessons ready for next day after dinner. I know——"

"Tais-toi, Lucy!" hissed Peony through her teeth. "Madame!"

"Donnez-moi cette grammaire, Marguerite, s'il vous plait," said Lucy, as Madame entered.

And I gave her the grammar, and we set to work again, full of envy for the domestic arrangements of Miss Martin's establishment during the dog days.

If there is a point on which Eleanor and I are quite agreed, among the many points we discuss and do not always agree upon, it is that of the need for a higher education for women. But ill as I think our sex provided for in this respect, and highly as I value good teaching, I would rather send a growing girl to a Miss Martin, even for fewer "educational advantages," and let her start in life with a sound, healthy constitution and a reasonable set of nerves, than have her head crammed and her health neglected under "the first masters," and so good an overseer as "Madame" to boot. For Madame certainly made us work, and was herself indefatigable.

The reckless imprudence of most girls in matters of health is proverbial, the wisdom of young matrons in this respect is not beyond reproach, and the lore which long and painful experience has given to older women is apt, like other lessons from that stern teacher, to come too late. It should at least avail to benefit their daughters, were it not that custom prescribes that they also should be kept in the dark till instructed in turn by the lamentable results of their ignorance, too often only when these are past repair.

Whether, though there are many things that women have no knowledge of, and many more of which their knowledge is superficial, their lack of learning on these points being erudition compared with their crass ignorance of the laws of health, the matter is again one of education; or whether it is an unfortunate development of a confusion between ignorance and innocence, and of mistaken notions of delicacy, who shall say? Unhappily, a studied ignorance of the ills that flesh is heir to is apt to bring them in double force about one's ears, and this kind of delicate-mindedness to bring delicacy of body in its train. Where it guides the counsels of those in charge of numbers of young people (as in Miss Mulberry's case), it is apt to result in the delicacy (more or less permanent) of several bodies.

But I am forgetting that I am not "preaching" to Eleanor by the kitchen fire, but writing my autobiography. I am forgetting, also, that I have not yet said who Miss Mulberry was.

CHAPTER XIV.

MISS MULBERRY—DISCIPLINE AND RECREATION—MADAME—CONVERSATION—ELEANOR'S OPINION OF THE DRAWING-MASTER—MISS ELLEN'S—ELEANOR'S APOLOGY.

Miss Mulberry was our school-mistress, and the head of the Bush House establishment. "Madame" was only a French mistress employed by Miss Mulberry, though she had more to do with the pupils than Miss Mulberry herself.

Miss Mulberry was stout, and I think by nature disposed to indolence, especially in warm weather. It was all the more creditable to her that she had worked hard for many years to support a paralytic mother and a delicate sister. The mother was dead now. Miss Ellen Mulberry, though an invalid, gave some help in teaching the younger ones; and Bush House had for so long been a highly-reputed establishment that Miss Mulberry was more or less prosperous, and could afford to keep a French governess to do the hard work.

Miss Mulberry was very conscientious, very kind-hearted, and the pink of propriety. Her appearance, at once bland and solid, produced a favourable impression upon parents and guardians. Being stout, and between fifty and sixty years old, she was often described as "motherly," though in the timidity, fidgetiness, and primness of her dealing with girls she was essentially a spinster.

Her good conscience and her timidity both helped to make her feel school-keeping a heavy responsibility, which should perhaps excuse the fact that we suffered at Bush House from an excess of the meddlesome discipline which seems to be *de rigueur* in girls' schools. I think Miss Mulberry would have felt that she had neglected her duty if we had ever been left to our own devices for an hour.

To growing girls, not too robust, leading sedentary lives, working very hard with our heads, and having (wholesome and sufficient meals, but) not as much animal food as most of us were accustomed to at home, the *nag* of never being free from supervision was both irritating and depressing. Much worse off were we than boys at school. No playing-fields had we; no leave could be obtained for country rambles by ourselves. Our dismal exercise was a promenade in double file under the eye and ear of Madame herself.

True, we were allowed fifteen minutes' "recreation" together, and by ourselves, in the school-room, just after dinner; but this inestimable privilege was always marred by the fact that Madame invariably came for us before the quarter of an hour had expired. No other part of school discipline annoyed us as this did. It had that element of injustice against which children always rebel. Why she did so remains to this day a puzzle to me. She worked very hard for her living—a fact which did not occur to us in those days to modify our view of her as our natural tormentor. In breaking faith with us daily by curtailing our allotted fifteen minutes of recreation, she deprived herself of rest to the exact amount by which she defrauded us.

She cannot have pined to begin to teach as soon as she had swallowed her food! I may do her an injustice, but the only reason I can think of as a likely one is that, by taking us unawares, she (I won't say hoped, but) expected to find us "in mischief."

It was a weak point of the arrangements of Bush House that Miss Mulberry left us so much to the care of Madame. Madame was twice as energetic as Miss Mulberry. Madame never spared herself if she never spared us. Madame was indefatigable, and in her own way as conscientious as Miss Mulberry herself. But Madame was not just, and she was not truthful. She had —either no sense at all, or—a quite different sense from ours of honour and uprightness. Perhaps the latter, for she seemed to break promises, tell lies, open letters, pry into drawers and boxes, and listen at keyholes from the highest sense of duty. And, which was even worse for us, she had no belief whatever in the trustworthiness of her pupils.

Miss Mulberry felt it to be her duty towards our parents and guardians to keep us under constant supervision; but Madame watched and worried us, I am convinced, in the persuasion that we were certain to get into mischief if we had the chance, and equally certain to do so deceitfully. She gave us full credit (I never could trace that she saw any discredit in deceit) for slyness in evading her authority, but flattered herself that her own superior slyness would maintain it in spite of us.

It vexed us all, but there were times when it irritated Eleanor almost to frenzy. She would have been in disgrace oftener and more seriously on the subject, but that Madame was a little afraid of her, and was, I think, not a little fond of her.

Madame was a clever woman, and a good teacher. She was sharp-witted, ready of tongue, and indefatigably industrious herself; and slow, stupid, or lazy girls found no mercy at her hands.

Eleanor's unusual abilities, the extent of her knowledge and reading on general subjects, the rapidity with which she picked up conversational French and wielded it in discussions with Madame, and finally her industry and perseverance, won Madame's admiration and good-will. I think she almost believed that Mademoiselle Arkwright's word was to be relied upon.

Eleanor never toadied her, which I fear we others (we were so utterly at her mercy!) did sometimes; assuming an interest we did not feel in her dissertations on the greatness of France and the character of her especial idol, the first Napoleon.

If Madame respected Eleanor, we school-girls almost revered her. "She talks so splendidly," Lucy said one day.

Not that the rest of us were by any means dumb. The fact that English was forbidden did not silence us, and on Sunday when (to Madame's undisguised chagrin) Miss Mulberry allowed us to speak English, we chattered like sparrows during an anthem. But Eleanor introduced a kind of talk which was new to most of us.

We could all chatter of people and places, and what was said on this occasion or what happened on another. We had one good mimic (Emma), and two or three of us were smart in description. We were observant of details and appearances, and we could one and all "natter" over our small grievances without wearying of the subject, and without ever speculating on their causes, or devising remedies for them.

But, with Eleanor, facts served more as points to talk from, than as talk in themselves. Through her influence the Why and How of things began to steal into our conversation. We had more discussion and less gossip, and found it better fun.

"One never tells you anything without your beginning to argue about it," said one of the girls to her one day.

"I'm very sorry," said poor Eleanor.

"You're very clever, you mean," said Emma. "What a lawyer you'd have made, Eleanor! While we growl at the Toad's tyranny, you make a case out of it."

(I regret to have to confess that, owing to a peculiarity of complexion, Madame was familiarly known to us, behind her back, as the Toad.)

"Well, I don't know," said Eleanor, puckering her brows and nursing her knees, as we all sat or lounged on the school-room floor, during the after-dinner recreation minutes, in various awkward but restful attitudes; "I can growl as well as anybody, but I never feel satisfied with bewailing over and over again that black's black. One wants to find out why it's black, and if anything would make it white. Besides, I think perhaps when one looks into one's grievances, one sees excuses for people—there are two sides to every question."

"There'll be one, two, three," said Emma, looking slowly round and counting the party with a comical imitation of Eleanor's thoughtful air —"there'll be fifteen sides to every question by the time we've all learnt to talk like you, my dear."

Eleanor burst out laughing, and we most of us joined her to such good purpose, that Madame overheard us, and thought it prudent to break up our sitting, though we had only had a short twelve minutes' rest.

Eleanor not only set the fashion of a more reasonable style of chat in our brief holiday hours, but she was apt to make lessons the subject of discussions which were at first resented by the other girls.

"I can't think," she began one day (it was a favourite way with her of opening a discussion)—"I can't think what makes Mr. Henley always make us put the shadows in in cobalt. Some shadows are light blue certainly, I think, especially on these white roads, but I don't think they are always; not in Yorkshire, at any rate. However, as far as that goes, he paints his things all in the same colours, whatever they're meant for; the Bay of Naples or the coast of Northumberland. By the bye, I know that I've heard that the shadows on the snow in Canada are really blue—bright blue."

"You're blue, deep blue," said Emma. "How you can talk shop out of lesson hours, Eleanor, I can't conceive. You began on grammar the other day, by way of enlivening our ten minutes' rest."

"I'm very sorry," said Eleanor: "I'm fond of drawing, you know."

"Oh, do let her talk, Emma!" cried Peony. "I do so like to hear her. Why are the shadows on the snow blue, Eleanor?"

"I can't think," said Eleanor, "unless it has something to do with reflection from the sky."

Eleanor was not always discreet enough to keep her opinion of Mr. Henley's style to herself and us. She was a very clever girl, and, like other very young people, her cleverness was apt to be aggressive; scorned compromises, and was not always sufficiently respectful towards the powers that be.

Her taste for drawing was known, and Madame taunted her one day with having a reputation for talent in this line, when her water-colour copies were not so effective as Lucy's; simply, I believe, with the wish to stimulate her to excel. I am sure Madame much preferred Eleanor to Lucy, as a matter of liking.

"Behold, Mademoiselle!" said she, holding up one of Lucy's latest copies, just glorified with a wide aureole of white cardboard "mounting"; "what do you think of this?"

"It is very like Mr. Henley's," said Eleanor warmly. "Lucy has taken great pains, I'm sure. It's quite as good as the copy, I think."

"But what do you think of it?" said Madame impatiently; she was too quick-witted to be easily "put off." "Is it not beautiful?"

"It is very smart, very gay," said Eleanor, who began to lose her temper. "All Mr. Henley's sketches are gay. The thatch on the house reminds me of the 'ends' of Berlin wool that are kept, after a big piece of work, for kettle-holders. The yellow tree and the blue tree are very pretty: there always is a yellow tree and a blue tree in Mr. Henley's sketches. I don't know what kind of trees they are. I never do. The trunks are pink, but that doesn't help one, for the markings on them are always the same."

Eleanor's French was quite good enough to give this speech its full weight, as Madame's kindling eyes testified. She flung the drawing from her, and was bursting forth into reply, when, by good luck, Miss Mulberry called for her so impatiently that she was obliged to leave the room.

I had been repeating a lesson to Miss Ellen Mulberry, who lay on a couch near the window, but we had both paused involuntarily to listen to Eleanor and Madame.

Miss Ellen was very good. She was also very gentle, and timid to nervousness. But from her couch she saw a good deal of the daily life of the school, and often understood matters better than those who were in the thick of it, I think.

When Madame had left the room, she called Eleanor to her, and in an almost trembling voice said:

"My dear, do you think you are quite right to speak so to Madame about that drawing?"

"I am very sorry, Miss Ellen," said Eleanor; "but it's what I think, and she asked me what I thought."

"You are very clever, my dear," said Miss Ellen, "and no one knows better than yourself that there are more ways than one of expressing one's opinion."

"Indeed," Eleanor broke in, "I don't want to be rude. I'm sorry I did speak so pertly. But oh, Miss Ellen, I wish you could see the trees my mother draws! How can I say I like those things of Mr. Henley's? Like green seaweeds on the end of a pink hay-fork! And we've lots of old etchings at home, with such trees in them! Like—well, like nothing but real trees and photographs."

Miss Ellen took Eleanor's hand and drew her towards her.

"My dear," said she, "you have plenty of sense; and have evidently used it to appreciate what your dear mother has shown and taught to you. Use it now, my dear, to ask yourself if it is reasonable to expect that men who could draw like the old masters would teach in ordinary girls' schools, or, if they would, that school-mistresses could afford to pay them properly without a much greater charge to the parents of pupils than they would be willing to bear. You have had great advantages at home, and have learnt enough to make you able to say very smart things; but fault-finding is an easy trade, my dear, and it would be wiser as well as kinder to see what good you can get from poor Mr. Henley's lessons, as to the use of the brush and colours, instead of neglecting your drawing because you don't like his style, which, after all, you needn't copy when you sketch from nature yourself. I will tell you, dear child, that my sister and I have talked this matter over before. Clever young people are apt to think that their stupid elders have never perceived what their brilliant young wits can put straight with half-a-dozen words. But I used to draw a little myself," continued Miss Ellen very modestly, "and I have never liked Mr. Henley's style. But he is such a very good old man, and so poor, that my sister has shrunk from changing. Still, of course our pupils are the first consideration, and we should have had another master if a much better one could have been got. But Mr. Markham, who is the only other one within reach, is not so painstaking and patient with his pupils as Mr. Henley; and though his style is rather better, it is not so very superior as to lead us, on the whole, to turn poor Mr. Henley away for him. As to Madame," said Miss Ellen, in conclusion, "she was quite right, my dear, to contrast your negligence with Lucy's industry, and your smart speech was not in good taste towards her, because you know that she knows nothing of drawing, and could not dispute the point with you. There she comes," added Miss Ellen rather nervously. She was afraid of Madame.

"I'll go and beg her pardon, dear Miss Ellen," said Eleanor penitently, and rushing out of the room, she met Madame in the passage, and we heard her pouring forth a torrent of apology and self-accusation in a style peculiar to herself. If in her youth and cleverness she was at times a little sharp-tongued and self-opinionated, the vehemence of her self-reproaches when she saw herself in fault was always a joke with those who knew her.

"Eleanor's confessions are only to be matched by her favourite Jeremy

Taylor's," said Jack one day.

"She's just as bumptious next time, all the same," said Clement. He had been disputing with Eleanor, and the generous grace of meeting an apology half-way was no part of his character.

He had an arbitrary disposition, in which Eleanor to some extent shared. He controlled it to fairness in discussions with men, but with men only. With Eleanor, who persisted in thinking for herself, and was not slow to express her thoughts, he had many hot disputes, in which he often seemed unable to be fair, and did not always trouble himself to be reasonable.

By his own account he "detested girls with opinions." Abroad he was politely contemptuous of feminine ideas; at home he was apt to be rudely so.

But this was only one, and a later development of many-sided Clement.

And the subject is a digression, and has no business here.

CHAPTER XV.

ELEANOR'S THEORIES REDUCED TO PRACTICE—STUDIES—THE ARITHMETIC-MASTER.

Madame was not ungenerous to an apology. She believed in Eleanor too, and was quite disposed to think that Eleanor might be in the right in a dispute with anybody but herself. Perhaps she hoped to hear her triumph in a discussion with Mr. Henley, or perhaps it was only as a punishment for her presumptuous remarks that Madame started the subject on the following day to the drawing-master himself.

"Miss Arkwright says your trees are all one, Mr. Henley," she began. (Madame's English was not perfect.) "Except that the half are yellow and the other half blue. She knows not the kind even."

The poor little drawing-master, who was at that moment "touching up" a yellow tree in one of the younger girls' copies, trying by skilfully distributed dabs to make it look less like a faded cabbage-leaf, blushed, and laid down his brush. Eleanor, who was just beginning to colour a copy of a mountain scene, turned scarlet, and let her first wash dry into unmanageable shapes as she darted indignant glances at Madame, who appeared to enjoy her bit of malice.

"Miss Arkwright will observe that these are sketches indicating the general effect of a scene; not tree studies."

"I know, Mr. Henley," said poor Eleanor, in much confusion; "at least, I mean I don't know anything about water-colour sketching, so I ought not to have said anything; and I never thought that Madame would repeat it. I was thinking of pencil-drawings and etchings; and I do like to know one tree from another," she added honestly.

"You draw in pencil yourself?" asked Mr. Henley.

"Oh no!" said Eleanor; "at least only a little. It was my mother's drawings I was thinking of; and how she used to show us the different ways of doing the foliage of different trees, and the marking on the bark of the trunks."

Mr. Henley drew a sheet of paper from his portfolio, and took a pencil from his case.

"Let us see, my dear young lady, what you remember of these lessons. The pencil is well cut. There are flat sides for shading, and sharp ends for outlines."

Madame's thin lips pursed with the ghost of a smile, as Eleanor, with hot cheeks and hands, came across "the room" to put her theories in practice.

"I can't do it, I know," she said, as she sat down, and gave herself one of those nervous twitches common to girls of the hobble-de-hoy age.

But Eleanor's nervous' spasms were always mitigated by getting something into her fingers. Pencil and paper were her favourite implements; and after a moment's pause, and a good deal of frowning, she said: "We've a good many oaks about us;" and forthwith began upon a bit of oak foliage.

"It's only a spray," she said.

"It's very good," said the drawing-master, who was now looking over her shoulder.

"Oak branches are all elbows," she murmured, warming to her work, and apparently talking to herself. "So different from willows and beeches."

"Ve-ry good," said Mr. Henley, as Eleanor fitted the branches dexterously into the clusters of leaves; "now for a little bit of the oak bark, if you please."

"This is only one tree, though," said Madame, who was also looking on. "Let us see others, mademoiselle."

"Willows are nice to do," said Eleanor, intent upon her paper; "and the bark is prettier than oak, I think, and easier with these long points. My mother says branches of trees should be done from the tips inwards; and they do fit in better, I think. Only willow branches seem as if they ought to be done outwards, they taper so. Beech trunks are very pretty, but the leaves are difficult, I think. Scotch pines are easy." And Eleanor left the beech and began upon the pine, fitting in the horizontal branches under the foliage groups with admirable effect.

"That will do, Miss Arkwright," said the little drawing-master. "Your mother has been a good guide to you; and Mother Nature will complete what she has begun. Now we will look at the copy, if you please."

Eleanor's countenance fell again. Her pink mountain had run into her blue mountain, and the interrupted wash had dried with hard and unmanageable outlines. Sponging was the only remedy.

Next drawing-lesson day Mr. Henley arrived a few minutes earlier than was his wont, staggering under a huge basket containing a large clump of flags and waterside herbage, which he had dug up "bodily," as he said. These he arranged on a tray, and then from the bottom of the basket produced the broken fragments of a red earthenware jug.

“It was such a favourite of mine, Miss Arkwright,” said he; “but what is sacred to a maid-of-all-work? My only consolation, when she smashed it this morning, was the thought that it would serve in the foreground of your sketch.”

Saying which, the kind-hearted little man laid the red crocks among the weeds, and after much pulling up and down of blinds to coax a good light on to the subject, he called Eleanor to set to work.

“It is *very* good of you,” said Eleanor emphatically. “When I have been so rude, too!”

“It is a pleasure,” said the old man; “and will be doubly so if you do it well. I should like to try it myself,” he added, making a few hasty dashes with the pencil. “Ah, my dear young lady, be thankful that you will sketch for pleasure, and not for bread! It is pleasanter to learn than to teach.”

Out of gratitude to Mr. Henley alone, Eleanor would have done her best at the new “study”; but apart from this the change of subject was delightful to her. She had an accurate eye, and her outlines had hitherto contrasted favourably with her colouring in copies of the sketches she could not like. The old drawing-master was delighted with her pencil sketch of his “crockery among the reeds,” and Eleanor confessed to getting help from him in the choice and use of her colours.

“Studies” became the fashion among the more intelligent pupils at Bush House; though I have heard that experience justified the old man’s prophecy that they would not be so popular with the parents as the former style had been. “They like lakes, and boats, and mountains, and ruins, and a brighter style of colouring,” he had said, and, as it proved, with truth.

Eleanor was his favourite pupil. Indeed, she was in favour with all the teachers.

A certain quaint little German was our arithmetic-master; a very good one, whose patience was often sorely tried by our stupidity or frivolity. On such occasions he rained epithets on us, which, from his imperfect knowledge of English, were often comical, and roused more amusement than shame. But for Eleanor he never had a harsh word. She was thoroughly fond of arithmetic, and “gave her mind to it,” to use a good old phrase.

“Ah!” the little man would yell at us. “You are so light-headed! Sometimes you do do a sum, and sometimes not; but you do never *think*. There is not one young lady of this establishment who thinks, but Miss Arkwright alone.”

I remember an incident connected with the arithmetic-master which occurred just after we came, and which roused Eleanor's intense indignation. It was characteristic, too, of Madame's ideas of propriety.

The weather was warm, and we were in the habit of dressing for tea. Our toilettes were of the simplest kind. Muslin garibaldis, for coolness, and our "second-best" skirts.

Eleanor, Matilda, and I shared one room. On the first Wednesday evening after our arrival at Bush House we were dressing as usual, when Emma ran in.

"I'm so sorry I forgot to tell you," said she; "you mustn't put on your muslin bodies to-night. The arithmetic-master is coming after tea."

"I don't understand," said Eleanor, who was standing on one leg as usual, and who paused in a struggle with a refractory elastic sandal to look up with a puckered brow, and general bewilderment. "What has the arithmetic to do with our dresses?"

Emma's saucy mouth and snub nose twitched with amusement, as she replied in exact mimicry of Madame's broken English: "Have you so little of delicacy as to ask, mademoiselle? Should the young ladies of this establishment expose their shoulders in the transparency of muslin to a professor?"

Matilda and I burst out laughing at Emma's excellent imitation of Madame; but Eleanor dropped her foot to the floor with a stamp that broke the sandal, and burst forth into an indignant torrent of words, which was only stayed by the necessity for resuming our morning dresses, and hastening down-stairs. There Eleanor swallowed her wrath with her weak tea; and I remember puzzling myself, to the neglect of mine, as to the probable connection between arithmetic-masters and transparent bodices.

CHAPTER XVI.

ELEANOR'S REPUTATION—THE MAD GENTLEMAN—FANCIES AND FOLLIES—MATILDA'S HEALTH—THE NEW DOCTOR.

We were not jealous of Eleanor's popularity. She was popular with the girls as well as with the teachers. If she was apt to be opinionated, she was candid, generous, and modest. She was always willing to help any one, and (the firmest seal of friendship!) she was utterly sincere.

She worked harder than any of us, so it was but just that she should be most commended. But of all who lagged behind her, and who felt Madame's severity, and created despair in the mind of the little arithmetic-master, the most unlucky was poor Matilda.

Matilda and I were now on the best of terms, and the credit of this happy condition of matters is more hers than mine.

It was not so much that I had learned more tact and sympathy (though I hope these qualities do ripen with years and better knowledge!) as because Matilda did most faithfully try to fulfil the good resolutions Major Buller's kindness had led her to make.

So far as Matilda's ailments were mental, I think that school-life may have been of some benefit.

Since the torments which have taught me caution in a household haunted by boys, I am less confidential with my diary than I used to be. And if I do not confide all my own follies to it, I am certainly not justified in recording other people's.

Not that Matilda makes any secret of the hero-worship she wasted on the man with the chiselled face and weird eyes, whom we used to see on the Riflebury Esplanade. She never spoke to him; but neither for that matter did his dog, a Scotch deerhound with eyes very like his master's, and a long nose which (uncomfortable as the position must have been) he kept always resting in his master's hand as the two paced up and down, hour after hour, by the sea.

What folly Miss Perry talked on the subject it boots not at this date to record. *I* never indulged a more fanciful feeling towards him than wonder, just dashed with a little fear—but I would myself have liked to know the meaning of that long gaze he and the dog sometimes turned on us!

We shall never know now, however, for the poor gentleman died in a lunatic asylum.

I hope, when they shut him up, that they found the deerhound guilty also of some unhydrophobiac madness, and imprisoned the two friends together!

Of course we laugh now about Matilda's fancy for the insane gentleman, though she declares that at the time she could never keep him out of her head —that if she had met him thirty-four successive times on the Esplanade, she would have borne no small amount of torture to earn the privilege of one more turn to meet him for the thirty-fifth—and that her rest was broken by waking dreams of the possible misfortunes which might account for his (and the dog's) obvious melancholy, and of impossible circumstances in which she should act as their good angel and deliverer.

At the time she kept her own counsel, and it was not because she had ever heard of the weird-eyed gentleman and his deerhound that Mrs. Minchin concluded her advice to Aunt Theresa on one occasion by a shower of nods which nearly shook the poppies out of her bonnet, and the oracular utterance —"She's got some nonsense or other into her head, depend upon it. Send her to school!"

One thing has often struck me in reading the biographies of great people. They must have to be written in quite a different way to the biographies of common people like ourselves.

For instance, when a practised writer is speaking of the early days of celebrated poets, he says quite gravely—"Like Byron, Scott, and other illustrious men, Hogg (the Ettrick shepherd) fell in love in his very early childhood." And of course it sounds better than if one said, "Like Smith, and Brown, and Jones, and nine out of every ten children, he did not wait for years of discretion to make a fool of himself."

Not being illustrious, Matilda blushes to remember this early folly; and not being a poet's biographer, Aunt Theresa said in a severe voice, for the general behoof of the school-room, that "Little girls were sometimes very silly, and got a great deal of nonsense into their heads." I do not think it ever dawned upon her mind that girls' heads not being jam-pots—which if you do not fill them will remain empty—the best way to keep folly out was to put something less foolish in.

She would have taken a great deal of trouble that her daughters might not be a flounce behind the fashions, and was so far-seeing in her motherly anxieties, that she junketed herself and Major Buller to many an entertainment, where they were bored for their pains, that an extensive acquaintance might ensure to the girls partners, both for balls and for life when they came to require them. But after what fashion their fancies should be shaped, or whether they had wholesome food and tender training for that high faculty of imagination by virtue of which, after all, we so largely love and hate, choose right or wrong, bear and forbear, adapt ourselves to the ups and downs of this world, and spur our dull souls to the high hopes of a better —anxiety on these matters Mrs. Buller had none.

As to Mrs. Minchin, she would not have known what it meant if it had been put in print for her to read.

Matilda's irritability was certainly repressed in public by school discipline, and from Eleanor's companionship our interests were varied and enlarged. But in spite of these advantages her health rapidly declined. And this without its seeming to attract Miss Mulberry's notice.

Indeed, she meddled very little in the matter of our health. She kept a stock of "family pills," which she distributed from time to time amongst us. They cured her headaches, she said; and she seemed rather aggrieved that they did not cure Matilda's.

But poor Matilda's headaches brought more than their own pain to her. They seemed to stupefy her, and make her quite incapable of work. Her complexion took a deadly, pasty hue, one eye was almost entirely closed, and to a superficial observer she perhaps did look—what Madame always pronounced her—sulky. Then, no matter how fully any lesson was at her fingers' ends, she stumbled through a series of childish blunders to utter downfall; and Madame's wrath was only equalled by her irony. To do Matilda justice, she often used almost incredible courage in her efforts to learn a task in spite of herself. Now and then she was successful in defying pain; but by some odd revenge of nature, what she learned in such circumstances was afterwards wiped as completely from her memory as an old sum is sponged from a slate.

To headache and backache, to vain cravings for more fresh air, and to an inequality of spirits and temper to which Eleanor and I patiently submitted, Matilda still added a cough, which seemed to exasperate Madame as much as her stupidity.

Not that our French governess was cruelly disposed. When she took Matilda's health in hand and gave her a tumbler of warm water every morning before breakfast, she did so in all good faith. It was a remedy that she used herself.

Poor Matilda was furious both with Madame's warm-water cure and Miss Mulberry's pill-box. She had a morbid hatred of being "doctored," which is often characteristic of chest complaints. She struggled harder than ever to work, in spite of her headaches; she ceased to complain of them, and concealed her cough to a great extent, by a process known amongst us as "smothering." The one remedy she pined for—fresh air—was the last that either Miss Mulberry or Madame considered appropriate to any form of a "cold."

This craving for fresh air helped Matilda in her struggle with illness. Our daily "promenade" was dull enough, but it was in the open air; and to be kept indoors, either as a punishment for ill-said lessons, or as a cure for her cough, was Matilda's great dread.

Night after night, when Madame had paid her final visit to our rooms, and we were safe, did Eleanor creep out of bed and noiselessly lower the upper sash of our window to please Matilda; whilst I sat (sometimes for an hour or more) upon the bolster of the bed in which Matilda and I slept together, and "nursed her head."

What quaint, pale, grave little maids we were! As full of aches and pains, and small anxieties, and self-repression, and tender sympathy, as any other daughters of Mother Eve.

Eleanor and I have often since said that we believe we should make excellent nurses for the insane, looking back upon our treatment of poor Matilda. We knew exactly when to be authoritative, and when to sympathize almost abjectly. I became skilful in what we called "nursing her head," which meant much more than that I supported it on my knees. Softly, but firmly, I stroked her brow and temples with both hands, and passed my fingers through her hair to the back of her head. I rarely failed to put her to sleep, and as she never woke when I laid her down, I have since suspected myself of unconscious mesmerism.

One night, when I had long been asleep, I was awakened by Matilda's hysterical sobs. She "couldn't get into a comfortable position;" her "back ached so." Our bed was very narrow, and I commonly lay so poised upon the outer edge to give Matilda room that more than once I have rolled on to the floor.

We spoke in undertones, but Eleanor was awake.

"Come and see if you can sleep with me, Margery," she said. "I lie very straight."

I scrambled out, and willingly crept in behind Eleanor, into her still narrower bed; and after tearful thanks and protestations, poor Matilda doubled herself at a restful angle, and fell asleep.

Happily for me, I was very well. Eleanor suffered from the utter change of mode of life a good deal; but she had great powers of endurance.

Fatigue, and "muddle on the brain," often hindered her at night from learning the lessons for next day. But she worked at them nevertheless; and tasks, that by her own account she "drove into her head" in bed, though she was quite unable to say them that evening, seemed to arrange themselves properly in her memory before the morning.

Matilda's ill-health came to a crisis at last. To smother a cough successfully, you must be able to escape at intervals. On one occasion the smothering was tried too long, and after the aggravated outburst which ensued, the doctor was called in. The Bush House family practitioner being absent, a new man came for him, who, after a few glances at Matilda, postponed the examination of her lungs, and begged to see Miss Mulberry.

Matilda had learned her last lesson in Bush House.

From the long interview with the doctor, Miss Mulberry emerged with a troubled face.

Lessons went irregularly that day. Our quarter of an hour's recreation was as much extended as it was commonly cut short, and Madame herself was subdued. She became a very kind nurse to Matilda, and crept many times from her bed during the night to see if "la pauvre petite" were sleeping, or had a wish that she could satisfy.

Indeed, an air of remorse seemed to tinge the kindness of the heads of Bush House to poor Matilda, which connected itself in Eleanor's mind with a brief dialogue that she overheard between Miss Mulberry and the doctor at the front door:

"I feel there has been culpable neglect," said Miss Mulberry mournfully. "But——"

"No, no. At least, not wilful," said the doctor; "and springing from the best motives. But I should not be doing my duty, madam, towards a lady in your responsible position, if I did not say that I have known too many cases in which the ill-results have been life-long, and some in which they have been rapidly fatal."

CHAPTER XVII.

ELEANOR'S HEALTH—HOLY LIVING—THE PRAYER OF THE SON OF SIRACH.

Matilda went home, and Eleanor and I remained at Bush House.

I fancy that when we no longer had to repress ourselves for poor Matilda's sake, Eleanor was more sensible of her own aches and pains. She also became rather irritable, and had more than one squabble with Madame about this time.

Eleanor had brought several religious books with her—books of prayers and other devotional works. They were all new to Matilda and me, and we began to use them, and to imitate Eleanor in various little devout customs.

On Sunday Eleanor used to read Jeremy Taylor's *Holy Living and Dying*; but as we never were allowed to be alone, she was obliged to bring it down-stairs. Unfortunately, the result of this was that Miss Mulberry, having taken it away to "look it over," pronounced it "not at all proper reading for young ladies," and it was confiscated. After this Eleanor reserved her devotional reading for bed-time, when, if she had got fairly through her lessons for next day, I was wont to read the Bible and other "good books" to her in a tone modulated so as not to reach Madame's watchful ear.

Once she caught us.

The books of Wisdom and Ecclesiasticus from the Apocrypha were favourite reading with Eleanor, who seemed in the grandly poetical praises of wisdom to find some encouragement under the difficulties through which we struggled towards a very moderate degree of learning. I warmly sympathized with her; partly because much of what I read was beautiful to read, even when I did not quite understand it; and partly because Eleanor had inspired me also with some of her own fervour against "the great war ofignorance."

But, as I said, Madame caught us at last.

Eleanor was lying, yet dressed, upon her bed, the window was open, and I, sitting cross-legged on the floor, was giving forth the prayer of the Son of Sirach, with (as I flattered myself) no little impressiveness. As the chapter went on my voice indiscreetly rose:

"When I was yet young, or ever I went astray, I desired wisdom openly in my prayer.

"I prayed for her before the temple, and will seek her out even to the end.

“Even from the flower till the grape was ripe hath my heart delighted in her: my foot went the right way, from my youth up I sought after her.

“I bowed down mine ear a little, and received her, and gat much learning.

* * * * * *

“Draw near unto me, ye unlearned, and dwell in the house of learning.

* * * * * *

“Put your neck under the yoke, and let your soul receive instruction: she is hard at hand to find.

“Behold with your eyes, how that I have had but little labour, and have gotten unto me much rest.

“Get learning——”

“Eh, mesdemoiselles! This is going to bed, is it? Ah! Give me that book, then.”

I handed over in much confusion the thin S.P.C.K. copy of the Apocrypha, bound in mottled calf, from which I had been reading; and ordering us to go to bed at once, Madame took her departure.

Madame could read English well, though she spoke it imperfectly. The next day she did not speak of the volume, and we supposed her to be examining it. Then Eleanor became anxious to get it back, and tried both argument and entreaty, for some time, in vain. At last Madame said:

“What is it, mademoiselle, that you so much wish to read in this volume of the holy writings?”

“Wisdom and Ecclesiasticus are what I like best,” said Eleanor.

“Eh bien!” said Madame, nodding her head like a porcelain Chinaman, and with a very knowing glance. “I will restore the volume, mademoiselle.”

She did restore it accordingly, with the historical narratives cut out, and many nods and grimaces expressive of her good wishes that we might be satisfied with it now.

In private, Eleanor stamped with indignation (whether or no her thick boots had fostered this habit I can’t say, but Eleanor was apt to stamp on occasion). We had our dear chapters again, however, and I promised Eleanor a new and fine copy of the mutilated favourite as a birthday present.

Eleanor was very good to me. She helped me with my lessons, and encouraged me to work. For herself, she laboured harder and harder.

I used to think that she was only anxious to get all the good she could out of the school, as she did not seem to have many so-called "advantages" at home, by her own account. But I afterwards found that she did just the same everywhere, strained her dark eyes over books, and absorbed information whenever and wherever she had a chance.

"I can't say you're fond of reading," said Emma one day, watching Eleanor as she sat buried in a book, "for I'm fond of reading myself, and we're not at all alike. I call you greedy!"

And Eleanor laughed, and quoted a verse from one of our favourite chapters: "They that eat me shall yet be hungry, and they that drink me shall yet be thirsty."

CHAPTER XVIII.

ELEANOR AND I ARE LATE FOR BREAKFAST—THE SCHOOL BREAKS UP—MADAME AND BRIDGET.

Eleanor and I overslept ourselves one morning. We had been tired, and when we did get up we hurried through our dressing, looking forward to fines and a scolding to boot.

But as we crept down-stairs we saw both the Misses Mulberry and Madame conversing together on the second landing. We felt that we were "caught," but to our surprise they took no notice of us; and as we went down the next flight we heard Miss Mulberry say, with a sigh, "Misfortunes never come alone."

We soon learnt what the new misfortune was. Poor Lucy had been taken ill. The doctor had been to see her early that morning, and had pronounced it fever—"Probably scarlet fever; and he recommends the school being broken up at once, as the holidays would soon be here anyway." So one of the girls told us.

Presently Miss Mulberry made her appearance; and we sat down to breakfast. She ate hers hurriedly, and then made a little speech, in which she begged us, as a personal favour, to be good; and if it was decided that we should go, to do our best to get our things carefully together, and to help to pack them.

I am sure we responded to the appeal. I wonder if it struck Madame, at this time, that it might be well to trust us a little more, as a rule? I remember Peony's saying, "Madame told me to help myself to tea. I might have taken two lumps of sugar, but I did not think it would be right."

We were all equally scrupulous; we even made a point of speaking in French, though Madame's long absences from the school-room, and the possibility of an early break-up for the holidays, gave both opportunity and temptation to chat in English.

On Monday evening at tea, Miss Mulberry made another little speech. The doctor had pronounced poor Lucy's illness to be scarlet fever, and we were all to be sent home the next day. There were to be no more lessons, and we were to spend the evening in packing and other preparations.

We were very sorry for poor Lucy, but we were young; and I do not think we could help enjoying the delights of fuss, the excitement of responsibility and packing, and the fact that the holidays had begun.

We were going in various directions, but it so happened that we all contrived to go by the same train to London. Some were to be dropped before we reached town; one lived in London; and Eleanor and I had to wait for half-an-hour before catching a train for the north.

For I was going to Yorkshire. The Arkwrights had asked me to spend the holidays with Eleanor. There was now nothing to be done but for us to go up together, all unexpected as we were.

How we packed and talked, and ran in and out of each other's rooms! It was late when we all got to bed that night.

Next morning the railway omnibus came for us, and with a curious sense of regret we saw our luggage piled up, and the little gate of Bush House close upon us.

As we moved off, Bridget, the nosegay-woman, drew near. Madame (who had shed tears as she bade us adieu) opened the gate again, ran out, cried shrilly to the driver to stop, and buying up half Bridget's basketful at one sweep, with more tears and much excitement, flung the flowers in amongst us. As she went backwards off the step, on to which she had climbed, she fell upon Bridget, who, with even more excitement and I think also with ready tears, clung to the already moving omnibus, and turned her basket upside down over our laps.

I have a dim remembrance of seeing her and Madame seem to fall over each other, or into each other's arms; and then, amid a shrill torrent of farewells and blessings in French and Irish, the omnibus rolled on, and Bush House was hid from our eyes.

CHAPTER XIX.

NORTHWARDS—THE BLACK COUNTRY—THE STONE COUNTRY.

We had a very noisy, happy journey to London. We chattered, and laughed, and hopped about like a lot of birds turned out of a cage. Emma sat by the window, and made a running commentary upon everybody and everything we passed in a strain of what seemed to us irresistible wit and humour. I fear that our conduct was not very decorous, but in the circumstances we were to be excused. The reaction was overwhelming.

Eleanor and I sobered down after we parted from the other girls, and thus became sensible of some fatigue and faintness. We had been too much excited to eat any of the bread-and-butter prepared for our early breakfast at Bush House. We had run up and down and stood on our feet about three times as much as need was; we had talked and laughed and shaken ourselves incessantly; we had put out our heads in the wind and sun as the train flew on; we had tried to waltz between the seats, and had eaten two ounces of "mixed sweets" given us by the housemaid, and deluged each other with some very heavy-scented perfume belonging to one of us.

After all this, Eleanor and I felt tired before our journey had begun. We felt faint, sick, anything but hungry, and should probably have travelled north in rather a pitiful plight, had not a motherly-looking lady, who sat in the waiting-room reading a very dirty book of tracts—and who had witnessed both our noisy parting from our companions and the subsequent collapse—advised us to go to the refreshment-room and get some breakfast. We yielded at last, out of complaisance towards her, and were rewarded by feeling wonderfully refreshed by a solid meal.

We laid in a stock of buns and chocolate lozenges for future consumption, and—thanks to Eleanor's presence of mind and experience—we got our luggage together, and started in the north train in a carriage by ourselves.

We talked very little now. Eleanor gazed out of her window, and I out of mine, in silence. As we got farther north, Eleanor's eyes dilated with a curious glow of pride and satisfaction. I had then no special attachment to one part of England more than another, but I had never seen so much of the country before, and it was a treat which did not lose by comparison with the limited range of our view at Bush House.

As we ran on, the bright, pretty, sociable-looking suburbs of London gave way to real country—beautiful, cared-for, garden-like, with grand timber, big houses, and grey churches, supported by the obvious parsonage and school; and deep shady lanes, with some little cart trotting quaintly towards the railway bridge over which we rushed, or boys in smock-frocks sitting on a gate, and shouting friendly salutations (as it seemed) to Eleanor and myself. Then came broad, fair pastures of fairy green, and slow winding rivers that we overtook almost before we had seen them, with ghostly grey pollard willows in formal mystical borders, contrasting with such tints of pale yellow and gay greens, which in their turn shone against low distances of soft blue and purple, that the sense of colour which my great-grandfather had roused in me made me almost tremble with a never-to-be-forgotten pleasure. From this flat but most fair country, the grey towers of Peterborough Cathedral stood up in ancient dignity; and then we ran on again. After a while the country became less rich in colour, and grander in form. No longer stretching flatly to low-lying distances of ethereal hue, it was broken into wooded hills, which folded one over the other with ever-increasing boldness of outline. Now and then the line ran through woods of young oak, with male ferns and bracken at their feet, where the wild hyacinths, which lie there like a blue mist in May, must for some weeks past have made way for the present carpet of pink campion.

And now the distance was no longer azure. Over the horizon and the lower part of the sky a thin grey veil had come—a veil of smoke. We were approaching the manufacturing districts. Grander and grander grew the country, less and less pure the colouring. The vegetation was rich almost to rankness; the well-wooded distances were heavily grey. Then tall chimneys poured smoke over the landscape and eclipsed the sun; and through strangely shaped furnaces and chimneys of many forms, which here poured fire from their throats like dragons, and there might have been the huge retorts and chemical apparatus of some giant alchemist, we ran into the station of a manufacturing town.

I gazed at the high blackened warehouses, chimneys, and furnaces, which loomed out of the stifling smoke and clanging noises, with horror and wonder.

"What a dreadful place!" I exclaimed. "Look at those dreadful things with flames coming out; and oh, Eleanor! there's fire coming out of the ground there. And look at that man opening that great oven door! Oh, what a fire! And what's he poking in it for? And do look! all the men are black. And what a frightful noise everything makes!"

Eleanor was looking all the time, but with a complacent expression. She only said, "It is a very busy place. I hear trade's good just now, too." And,

"You should see the furnaces at night, Margery, lighting up all the hills. It's grand!"

As she sniffed up the smoke with, I might almost say, relish, I felt that she did not sympathize with my disgust. But any discussion on the subject was stopped by our having to change carriages, and we had just settled ourselves comfortably once more, when I got a bit of iron "filings" into my eye. It gave me a good deal of pain and inconvenience, and by the time that I could look out of the window again, we had left the black town far behind. The hills were almost mountains now, and sloped away on all sides of us in bleak and awful grandeur. The woodlands were fewer; we were on the moors. Only a few hours back we had been amongst deep hedges and shady lanes, and now for hedges we had stone walls, and for deep embowered lanes we could trace the unsheltered roads, gleaming as they wound over miles of distant hills. Deep below us brawled a river, with here and there a gaunt mill or stone-built hamlet on its banks.

I had never seen any country like this; and if I had been horrified by the black town, my delight with the noble scenery beyond it was in proportion. I stood at the open window, with the moor breeze blowing my hair into the wildest elf-locks, rapturously excited as the great hills unfolded themselves and the shifting clouds sent shifting purple shadows over them. Very dark and stern they looked in shade, and then, in a moment more, the cloud was past, and a broad smile of sunshine ran over their face, and showed where cultivation was creeping up the hillside and turning the heather into fields.

Eleanor leaned out of the window also. Excitement, which set me chattering, always made her silent. But her parted lips, distended nostrils, and the light in her eyes bore witness to that strange power which hill country sways over hill-born people. To me it was beautiful, but to her it was home. I better understood now, too, her old complaints of the sheltered (she called it *stuffy*) lane in which we walked two and two when we "went into the country" at school. She used to rave against the park palings that hedged us in thing is to slave—to work hard at it. At least, not merely hard-working, but to go a at least to be herself somewhere where "one could see a few miles about one, and breathe some wind."

As we stood now, drinking in the breeze, I think the same thought struck us both, and we exclaimed with one voice: "Poor Matilda! How she would have enjoyed this!"

We next stopped at a rather dreary-looking station, where we got out, and Eleanor got our luggage together, aided by a porter who seemed to know her, and whom she seemed to understand, though his dialect was unintelligible to me.

"I suppose we must have a cab," said Eleanor, at last. "They don't expect us."

"*Tommusisinttarn,*" said the porter suggestively; which, being interpreted, meant, "Thomas is in the town."

"To be sure, for the meat," said Eleanor. "The dog-cart, I suppose?"

"And t'owd mare," added the porter.

"Well, the boxes must come by the carrier. Come along, Margery, if you don't mind a little bit of walking. We must find Thomas. We have to send down to the town for meat," she added.

We found Thomas in the yard of a small inn. He was just about to start homewards.

By Eleanor's order, Thomas lifted me into the dog-cart, and then, to my astonishment, asked "Miss Eleanor" if she would drive. Eleanor nodded, and, climbing on to the driver's seat, took the reins with reassuring calmness. Thomas balanced the meat-basket behind, and "t'owd mare" started at a good pace up a hill which would have reduced most south-country horses to crawl.

"Father and Mother are away still," said Eleanor, after a pause. "So Thomas says. But they'll be back in a day or two."

We were driving up a sandy road such as we had seen winding over the hills. To our left there was a precipitous descent to the vale of the river. To our right, flowers, and ferns, and heather climbed the steep hill, broken at every few yards by tiny torrents of mountain streams. The sun was setting over the distant Deadmanstone moors; little dropping wells tinkled by the roadside, where dozens of fat black snails were out for an evening stroll, and here and there a brimming stone trough reflected the rosy tints of the sky.

It was grey and chilly when we drove into the village. A stone pack-horse track, which now served as footpath, had run by the road and lasted into the village. The cottages were of stone, the walls and outhouses were of stone, and the vista was closed by an old stone church, like a miniature cathedral. There was more stone than grass in the churchyard, and there were more loose stones than were pleasant on the steep hill, up which we scrambled before taking a sharp turn into the Vicarage grounds.

CHAPTER XX.

THE VICARAGE—KEZIAH—THE DEAR BOYS—THE COOK—A YORKSHIRE TEA—BED-FELLOWS.

It was Midsummer. The heavy foliage brushed our faces as "the old mare," with slack reins upon her back, drew us soberly up the steep drive, and stood still, of her own accord, before a substantial-looking house, built—"like everything else," I thought—of stone. Huge rose-bushes—literal *bushes*, not "dwarfs" or "standards"—the growth of many years, bent under their load of blossoms. The old "maiden's blush," too rare now in our bedding plant gardens, the velvety "damask," the wee Scotch roses, the prolific white, and the curious "York and Lancaster," with monster moss-rose trees, hung over the carriage-road. The place seemed almost overgrown with vegetation, like the palace of the Sleeping Beauty.

As we turned the corner towards the house, Eleanor put out her left hand and dragged off a great branch of "maiden's blush." She forgot the recoil, which came against my face. All the full-blown flowers shed their petals over me, and I made my first appearance at the Vicarage covered with rose-leaves.

It was Keziah who welcomed us, and I have always had an affection for her in consequence. She was housemaid then, and took to the kitchen afterwards. After she had been about five years at the Vicarage, she announced one day that she wished to go. She had no reason to give but that she "thought she'd try a change." She tried one—for a month—and didn't like it. Mrs. Arkwright took her back again, and in kitchen and back premises she reigns supreme to this day.

From her we learned that Mr. and Mrs. Arkwright, who had gone away for a parson's fortnight, were still from home. We had no lack of welcome, however.

It seems strange enough to speak of a fire as comfortable in July. And yet I well remember that the heavy dew and evening breeze was almost chilly after sunset, and a sort of vault-like feeling about the rooms, which had been for a week or more unused, made us offer no resistance when Keziah began to light a fire. While she was doing so Eleanor exclaimed, "Let's go and warm ourselves in the kitchen."

Any idea of comfort connected with a kitchen was quite new to me, butI followed Eleanor, and made my first acquaintance with the old room where we have spent so many happy hours.

We found the door shut; much, it seemed, to Eleanor's astonishment. But the reason was soon evident. As our footsteps sounded on the stone passage there arose from behind the kitchen door an utterly indescribable din of howling, yowling, squealing, scratching, and barking.

"It's the dear boys!" said Eleanor, and she ran to open the door. For a moment I thought of her brothers (who must, obviously, be maniacs!), but I soon discovered that the "dear boys" were the dogs of the establishment, who were at once let loose upon us *en masse*. I have a faint remembrance of Eleanor and a brown retriever falling into each other's arms with cries of delight; but I was a good deal absorbed by the care of my own small person, under the heavy onslaught of dogs big and little. I was licked copiously from chin to forehead by the more impetuous, and smelt threateningly at the calves of my legs by the more cautious of the pack.

They were subsiding a little, when Eleanor said, "Oh, cook, why did you shut them up? Why didn't you let them come and meet us?"

"And how was I to know who it was at the door, Miss Eleanor?" replied an elderly, stern-looking female, who, in her time, ruled us all with a rod of iron, the dogs included. "Dear knows it's not that I want them in the kitchen. The way them dogs behaves, Miss Eleanor, is *scandilus*."

"Dear boys!" murmured Eleanor; on which all the dogs, who were settling down to sleep on the hearth, wagged their tails, and threatened to move.

"Much good it is me cleaning," cook continued, "when that great big brown beast of yours goes roaming about every night in the shrubberies, and comes in with his feet all over my clean floor."

"It makes rather pretty marks, I think," said Eleanor; "like pot-moulding, only not white. But never mind, you've me at home now to wipe their paws."

"They've missed you sorely," said the cook, who seemed to be softening. "I almost think they knew it was you, they were so mad to get out."

"Dear boys!" cried Eleanor, once more; and the dogs, who were asleep now, wagged their tails in their dreams.

"And there's more's missed you than them," cook continued. "But, bless us, Miss Eleanor, you don't look much better for being in strange parts. That young lady, too, looks as if she enjoyed poor health. Well, give me native air, there's nothing like it; and you've not got back to yours too soon."

Eleanor threw her arms round the cook, and danced her up and down the kitchen.

"Oh, dear cookey!" she cried; "I am so glad to be back again. And do be kind to us, and give us tea-cakes, and brown bread toast, and let the dogs come in to tea."

Cook pushed her away, but with a relenting face.

"There, there, Miss Eleanor. Take that jug of hot water with you, and take the young lady up-stairs; and when you've cleaned yourselves, I'll have something for you to eat; and you may suit yourselves about the dogs,—I'm sure I don't want them. You've not got so much more sensible with all your schooling," she added.

We went off to do her bidding, and left her muttering, "And what folks as can edicate their own children sends 'em all out of the house for, passes me; to come back looking like a damp handkerchief, with dear knows what cheap living and unwholesome ways, and want of native air."

Cook's bark was worse than her bite.

"She gives the dear boys plenty to eat," said Eleanor; and she provided for us that evening in the same liberal spirit.

What a feast we had! Strong tea, and abundance of sugar and rich cream. We laid the delicious butter on our bread in such thick clumps, that sallow-faced Madame would have thought us in peril of our lives. There was brown bread toast, too; and fried ham and eggs, and moor honey, and Yorkshire tea-cakes. In the middle of the table Keziah had placed a large punch-bowl, filled with roses.

And all the dogs were on the hearth, and they all had tea with us.

After tea we tried to talk, but were so sleepy that the words died away on our heavy lips. So we took Keziah's advice and went to bed.

"Keziah has put the chair-bed into my room, Margery dear," said Eleanor.

"I am so glad," said I. "I would rather be with you."

"Would you like a dog to sleep with you?" Eleanor politely inquired. "I shall have Growler inside, and my big boy outside. Pincher is a nice little fellow; you'd better have Pincher."

I took Pincher accordingly, and Pincher took the middle of the bed.

We were just dropping off to sleep when Eleanor said, "If Pincher snores, darling, hit him on the nose."

"All right," said I. "Good-night." I had begun a confused dream, woven from my late experiences, when Eleanor's voice roused me once more.

“Margery dear, if Growler *should* get out of my bed and come on to yours, mind you kick him off, or he and Pincher will fight through the bed-clothes.”

But whether Pincher did snore, or Growler invade our bed, I slept much too soundly to be able to tell.

CHAPTER XXI.

GARDENING—DRINKINGS—THE MOORS—WADING—BATRACHOSPERMA—THE CHURCH—LITTLE MARGARET.

Both Eleanor and I were visited that night by dreams of terrible complications with the authorities at Bush House. It was a curious relief to us to wake to clear consciences and the absolute control of our own conduct for the day.

It took me several minutes fairly to wake up and realize my new position. The window being in the opposite direction (as regarded my bed) from that of our room at Miss Mulberry's, the light puzzled me, and I lay blinking stupidly at a spray of ivy that had poked itself through the window as if for shelter from the sun, which was already blazing outside. Pincher brought me to my senses by washing my face with his tongue; which I took all the kindlier of him that he had been, of all the dear boys, the most doubtful about the calves of my legs the evening before.

As we dressed, I adopted Eleanor's fashion of doing so on foot, that I might examine her room. As is the case with the "bowers" of most English country girls of her class, it was rich in those treasures which, like the advertised contents of lost pocket-books, are "of no value to any one but the owner." Prints of sacred subjects in home-made frames, knick-knacks of motley variety, daguerreotypes and second-rate photographs of "the boys"—*i. e.* Clement and Jack—at different ages, and of "the dear boys" also. "All sorts of things!" as I exclaimed admiringly. But Eleanor threatened at last to fine me if I did not get dressed instead of staring about me, so we went down-stairs, and had breakfast with the dogs.

"The boys will be home soon," said Eleanor, as we devoured certain plates of oatmeal porridge, which Keziah had provided, and which I tasted then for the first time. "I must get their gardens tidied up before they come. Shall you mind helping me, Margery?"

The idea delighted me, and after breakfast we tied on our hats, rummaged out some small tools from the porch, and made our way to the children's gardens. They were at some little distance from the big flower-garden, and the path that led to them was heavily shaded by shrubbery on one side, and on the other by a hedge which, though "quickset" as a foundation, was now a mass of honeysuckle and everlasting peas. The scent was delicious.

From this we came out on an open space at the top of the kitchen garden, where, under a wall overgrown with ivy, lay the children's gardens.

"What a wilderness!" was Eleanor's first exclamation, in a tone of dismay, and then she added with increased vehemence, "He's taken away the rhubarb-pot. What will Clement say?"

"What is it, dear?" I asked.

"It's the rhubarb-pot," Eleanor repeated. "You know Clement is always having new fads every holidays, and he can't bear his things being disturbed whilst he's at school. But how can I help it if I'm at school too?"

"Of course you can't," said I, gladly seizing upon the only point in her story that I could understand, to express my sympathy.

"And he got one of the rhubarb-pots last holidays," Eleanor continued. "It was rather broken, and Thomas gave in to his having it then, so it's very mean of him to have moved it now, and I shall tell him so. And Clement painted church windows on it, and stuck it over a plant of ivy at the top of the garden. He thought it would force the ivy, and he expected it would grow big by the time he came home. He wanted it to hang over the top, and look like a ruin. Oh, he will be so vexed!"

The ivy plant was alive, though the "ruin" had been removed by the sacrilegious hands of Thomas. I suggested that we should build a ruin of stones, and train the ivy over that, which idea was well received by Eleanor; the more so that a broken wall at the top of the croft supplied materials, and Stonehenge suggested itself as an easy, and certainly respectable, model.

Meanwhile we decided to "do the weeding first," as being the least agreeable business, and so set to work; I in a leisurely manner, befitting the heat of the day, and Eleanor with her usual energy. She toiled without a pause, and accomplished about treble the result of my labours. After we had worked for a long time, she sat up, pressing her hand to her forehead.

"My head quite aches, Margery, and I'm so giddy. It's very odd; gardening never made me so before I went away."

"You work so at it," said I, "you may well be tired. What makes you work so at things?"

"I don't know," said Eleanor, laughing. "Cook says I do foy at things so. But when one once begins, you know——"

"What's *foy*?" I interrupted. "Cook says you foy—what does she mean?"

"Oh, to foy at anything is to slave—to work hard at it. At least, not merely hard-working, but to go at it very hotly, almost foolishly; in fact, to foy at it, you know. Clement foys at things too. And then he gets tired and cross; and so do I, often. What o'clock is it, Margery?"

I pulled out my souvenir watch and answered, "Just eleven."

"We ought to have some 'drinkings,' we've worked so hard," said Eleanor, laughing again. "Haymakers, and people like that, always have drinkings at eleven, you know, and dinner at one, and tea at four or five, and supper at eight. Ah! there goes Thomas. Thomas!"

Thomas came up, and Eleanor (discreetly postponing the subject of the rhubarb-pot for the present) sent a pleading message to cook, which resulted in her sending us two bottles of ginger-beer and several slices of thick bread-and-butter. The dear boys, who had been very sensibly snoozing in the shade, divined by some instinct the arrival of our lunch-basket, and were kind enough to share the bread-and-butter with us.

"Drinkings" over, we set to work again.

I was surprised to observe that there were four box-edged beds, but as Eleanor said nothing about it, I made no remark. Perhaps it belonged to some dead brother or sister.

As the weeds were cleared away, one plant after another became apparent. I called Eleanor's attention to all that I found, and she seemed to welcome them as old friends.

"Oh, that's the grey primrose; I'm so glad! And there are Jack's hepaticas; they look like old rubbish. Don't dig deep into Jack's garden, please, for he's always getting plants and bulbs given him by people in the village, and he sticks everything in, so his garden really is crammed full; and you're sure to dig into tulips, or crocuses, or lilies, or something valuable."

"Doesn't Clement get things given him?" said I.

"Oh, he has plenty of plants," said Eleanor, "but then he's always making great plans about his garden; and the first step towards his improvements is always to clear out all the old things, and make what he calls 'a clean sweep of the rubbish.'"

By the time that the "twelve o'clock bell" rang from the church-tower below, the heat was so great that we gathered up our tools and went home.

In the afternoon Eleanor said, "Were you ever on the moors? Did you ever wade? Do you care about water-weeds? Did you ever eat bilberries, or carberries?—but they're not ripe yet. Shall we go and get some Batrachosperma, and paddle a bit, and give the dear boys a bathe?"

"Delightful!" said I; "but do you go out alone?"

“What should we take anybody with us for?” said Eleanor, opening her eyes.

I could not say. But as we dressed I said, “I’m so glad you don’t wear veils. Matilda and I used to have to wear veils to take care of our complexion.”

Eschewing veils and every unnecessary encumbrance, we set forth, followed by the dogs. I had taken off my crinoline, because Eleanor said we might have to climb some walls, and I had borrowed a pair of her boots, because my own were so uncomfortable from being high-heeled and narrow-soled. They were too thin for stony roads also, and, though they were prettily ornamented, they pinched my feet.

We went upwards from the Vicarage along hot roads bordered by stone walls. At last we turned and began to go downwards, and as we stood on the top of the steep hill we were about to descend, Eleanor, with some pride in her tone, asked me what I thought of the view.

It was very beautiful. The slopes of the purple hills were grand. I saw “moors” now.

“The best part of it is the air, though,” she said.

The air was, in fact, wind; but of a dry, soft, exhilarating kind. It seemed to get into our heads, and we joined hands and ran wildly down the steep hill together.

“What fun!” Eleanor cried, as we paused to gain breath at the bottom. “Now you’ve come there’ll be four of us to run downhill. We shall nearly stretch across the road.”

At last we came to a stone bridge which spanned the river. It was not a very wide stream, and it was so broken with grey boulders, and clumps of rushes and overhanging ferns, that one only caught sight of the water here and there, in tiny torrents and lakes among the weeds.

My delight was boundless. I can neither forget nor describe those first experiences of real country life, when Eleanor and I rambled about together. I think she was at least as happy as I, and from time to time we both wished with all our hearts that “the other girls” could be there too. The least wisely managed of respectable schools has this good point, that it enlarges one’s sympathies and friendships!

We wandered some little way up the Ewden, as Eleanor called the river, and then, coming to a clear, running bit of stream, with a big grey boulder on the bank hard by to leave our shoes and stockings on, we took these off, and also our hats, and, kilting up our petticoats, plunged bravely into the stream.

"Wet your head!" shouted Eleanor; and following her example, as well as I could for laughing, and for the needful efforts to keep my feet, I dabbled my head liberally with water scooped up in the palms of my hands.

"Oh!" I cried, "how strong the water is, and how deliciously cold it is! And oh, look at the little fishes! They're all round my feet. And oh, Eleanor, call the dogs, they're knocking me down! How hard the stones are, and oh, how slippery!"

I fell against a convenient boulder, and Eleanor turned back, the dogs raging and splashing around her.

"I hope you're not treading on the Batrachosperma?" she said, anxiously.

"What is it?" I cried.

"It's what I've chiefly come in for," said she. "I want some to lay out. It's a water-weed; a fresh-water alga, you know, like seaweed, only a fresh-water plant. I'm looking for the stone it grew near. Oh, that's it you're on! Climb up on to it out of the way, Margery dear. It's rather a rare kind of weed, and I don't want it to be spoiled. Call the dogs, please. Oh, look at all the bits they've broken off!"

Eleanor dodged and darted to catch certain fragments of dark-looking stuff that were being whirled away. With much difficulty she caught two or three, and laid one of them in my hand. But I was not prepared for the fact that it felt like a bit of jelly, and it slipped through my fingers before I had time to examine the beauty of the jointed branches pointed out by Eleanor, and in a moment more it was hopelessly lost. We put what we had got into some dock-leaves for safety, and having waded back to our stockings, we put on our hats and walked barefoot for a few yards through the heather, to dry our feet, after which we resumed our boots and stockings and set off homewards.

"We'll go by the lower road," said Eleanor, "and look at the church."

For some time after Eleanor had passed in through the rickety gates of the south porch, I lingered amongst the gravestones, reading their quaint inscriptions. Quaint both in matter and in the manner of rhyme and spelling. As I also drew towards the porch, I looked up to see if I could tell the time by the dial above it. I could not, nor (in spite of my brief learning in Dr. Russell's grammar) could I interpret the Latin motto, "*Fugit Hora. Ora*"—"The hour flies. Pray."

As I came slowly and softly up the aisle, I fancied Eleanor was kneeling, but a strange British shame of prayer made her start to her feet and kept me from kneeling also; though the peculiar peace and devout solemnity which seemed to be the very breath of that ancient House of God made me long to do something more expressive of my feelings than stand and stare.

There was no handsome church at Riflebury; the one the Bullers "attended" when we were at the seaside was new, and not beautiful. The one Miss Mulberry took us to was older, but uglier. I had never seen one of these old parish churches. This cathedral among the moors, with its massive masonry, its dark oak carving, its fragments of gorgeous glass, its ghostly hatchments and banners, and its aisles paved with the tombstones of the dead, was a new revelation.

I was silent awhile in very awe. I think it was a bird beginning to chirp in the roof which made me dare to speak, and then I whispered, "How quiet it is in here, and how cool!"

I had hardly uttered the words when a flash of lightning made me start and cry out. A heavy peal of thunder followed very quickly.

"Don't be frightened, Margery dear," said Eleanor; "we have very heavy storms here, and we had better go home. But I am so glad you admire our dear old church. There was one very hot Sunday last summer, when a thunderstorm came on during Evening Prayer. I was sitting in the choir, where I could see the storm through the south transept door, and the great stones in the transept arches. It was so cool in here, and all along I kept thinking of 'a refuge from the storm, a shadow in the heat,' and 'a great rock in a weary land.'"

As we sat together at tea that evening, Eleanor went back to the subject of the church. I made some remark about the gravestones in the aisles, and she said, "Next time we go in, I want to show you one of them in the chancel."

"Who is buried there?" I asked.

"My grandfather, he was vicar, you know, and my aunt, who was sixteen. (My father has got the white gloves and wreath that were hung in the church for her. They always used to do that for unmarried girls.) And my sister; my only sister—little Margaret."

I could not say anything to poor Eleanor. I stroked her head softly and kissed it.

"One thing that made me take to you," she went on, "was your name being Margaret. I used to think she might have been like you. I have so wished I had a sister. The boys are very dear, you know; but still boys think about themselves, of course, and their own affairs. One has more to run after them, you know. Not that any boys could be better than ours, but—anyway, Margery darling, I wish you weren't here just on a visit, but were going to stop here always, and be my sister!"

"So do I!" I cried. "Oh! so very much, Eleanor!"

CHAPTER XXII.

A NEW HOME—THE ARKWRIGHTS' RETURN—THE BEASTS—GOING TO MEET THE BOYS—JACK'S HATBOX—WE COME HOME A RATTLER.

It is not often (out of a fairy tale) that wishes to change the whole current of one's life are granted so promptly as that wish of mine was.

The next morning's post brought a letter from Mrs. Arkwright. They were staying in the south of England, and had seen the Bullers, and heard all their news. It was an important budget. They were going abroad once more, and it had been arranged between my two guardians that I was to remain in England for my education, and that my home was to be—with Eleanor. Matilda was to go with her parents; to the benefit, it was hoped, of her health. Aunt Theresa sent me the kindest messages, and promised to write to me. Matilda sent her love to us both.

"And the day after to-morrow they come home!" Eleanor announced.

When the day came we spent most of it in small preparations and useless restlessness. We filled all the flower vases in the drawing-room, put some of the choicest roses in Mrs. Arkwright's bedroom, and made ourselves very hot in hanging a small union-jack which belonged to the boys out of our own window, which looked towards the high-road. Eleanor even went so far as to provoke a severe snub from the cook, by offering suggestions as to the food to be prepared for the travellers.

The dogs fully understood that something was impending, and wandered from room to room at our heels, sitting down to pant whenever we gave them a chance, and emptying the water jug in Mr. Arkwright's dressing-room so often that we were obliged to shut the door when Keziah had once more filled the ewer.

About half-an-hour after the curfew bell had rung the cab came. The dogs were not shut up this time, and they, and we, and the Arkwrights met in a very confused and noisy greeting.

"God bless you, my dear!" I heard Mr. Arkwright say very affectionately, and he added almost in the same breath, "Do call off the dogs, my dear, or else take your mother's beasts."

I suppose Eleanor chose the latter alternative, for she did not call off the dogs, but she took away two or three tin cans with which Mr. Arkwright was laden, and which had made him look like a particularly respectable milkman.

"What are they?" she asked.

"Crassys," said Mrs. Arkwright, with apparent triumph in her tone, "and Serpulæ, and two Chitons, and several other things."

I thought of Uncle Buller's "collection," and was about to ask if the new "beasts" were insects, when Eleanor, after a doubtful glance into the cans, said, "Have you brought any fresh water?"

Mrs. Arkwright pointed triumphantly to a big stone-bottle cased in wickerwork, under which the cabman was staggering towards the door. It looked like spirits or vinegar, but was, as I discovered, seawater for the aquarium. With this I had already made acquaintance, having helped Eleanor to wipe the mouths of certain spotted sea anemones with a camel's-hair brush every day since my arrival.

"The Crassys are much more beautiful," she assured me, as we helped Mrs. Arkwright to find places for the new-comers. "We call them Crassys because their name is Crassicornis. I don't believe they'll live, though, they are so delicate."

"I rather think it may be because being so big they get hurt in being taken off the rocks," said Mrs. Arkwright, "and we were very careful with these."

"I'm *afraid* the Serpulæ won't live!" said Eleanor, gazing anxiously with puckered brows into the glass tank.

Mrs. Arkwright was about to reply, when the dogs burst into the room, and, after nearly upsetting both us and the aquarium, bounded out again.

"Dear boys!" cried Eleanor. And "Dear boys!" murmured Mrs. Arkwright from behind the magnifying glass, through which she was examining the "beasts."

"I wonder what they're running in and out for?" said I.

The reason proved to be that supper was ready, and the dogs wanted us to come into the dining-room. Mr. Arkwright announced it in more sedate fashion, and took me with him, leaving Eleanor and her mother to follow us.

"In three days more," said Eleanor, as we sat down, "the boys will be here, and then we shall be quite happy."

Eleanor and I were as much absorbed by the prospect of the boys' arrival as we had been by the coming of her parents.

We made a "ruin" at the top of the little gardens, which did not quite fulfil our ideal when all was done, but we hoped that it would look better when the ivy was more luxuriant. We made all the beds look very tidy. The fourth bed was given to me.

"Now you *are* our sister!" Eleanor cried. "It seems to make it so real now you have got *her* bed."

We thoroughly put in order the old nursery, which was now "the boys' room," a proceeding in which Growler and Pincher took great interest, jumping on and off the beds, and smelling everything as we set it out. Growler was Clement's dog, I found, and Pincher belonged to Jack.

"They'll come in a cab, because of the luggage," said Eleanor, "and because we are never quite sure when they will come; so it's no use sending to meet them. They often miss trains on purpose to stay somewhere on the road for fun. But I think they'll come all right this time—I begged them to—and we'll go and meet them in the donkey-carriage."

The donkey-carriage was a pretty little thing on four wheels, with a seat in front and a seat behind, each capable of holding one small person. Eleanor had almost outgrown the front seat, but she managed to squeeze into it, and I climbed in behind. We had dressed Neddy's head and our own hats liberally with roses, so that our festive appearance drew the notice of the villagers, more than one of whom, from their cottage-doors, asked if we were going to meet "the young gentlemen," and added, "They'll be rare and glad to get home, I reckon!"

Impatience had made us early, and we drove some little distance before espying the cab, which toiled uphill at much the same pace as the black snails crawled by the roadside. Eleanor drew up by the ditch, and we stood up and waved our handkerchiefs. In a moment two handkerchiefs were waving from the cab-windows. We shouted, and faint hoorays came back upon the breeze. Neddy pricked his ears, the dogs barked, and only the cabman remained unmoved, though we could see sticks and umbrellas poked at him from within, in the vain effort to induce him to hasten on.

At last we met. The boys tumbled out, one on each side, and a good deal of fragmentary luggage tumbled out after them. Clement seemed to be rather older than Eleanor, and Jack, I thought, a little younger than me.

"How d'ye do, Margery?" said Jack, shaking me warmly by the hand. "I'm awfully glad to hear the news about you; we shall be all square now, two and two, like a quadrille."

"How do you do, Miss Vandaleur?" said Clement.

"Look here, Eleanor," Jack broke in again; "I'll drive Margery home in the donkey-carriage, and you can go with Clem in the cab. I wish you'd give me the wreath off your hat, too."

Eleanor willingly agreed, the wreath was adjusted on Jack's hat, and we were just taking our places, when he caught sight of the luggage that had fallen out on Clement's side of the cab—some fishing-rods, a squirrel in a fish-basket, and a hat-box.

"Oh!" he screamed, "there's my hat-box! Take the reins, Margery!" and he flew over the wheel, and returned, hat-box in hand.

"Is it a new hat?" I asked sympathizingly.

"A hat!" he scornfully exclaimed. "My hat's loose in the cab somewhere, if it came at all; but all my beetles are in here, pinned to the sides. Would you mind taking it on your knee, to be safe?"

And having placed it there, he scrambled once more into the front seat, and we were about to start (the cab was waiting for us, the cabman looking on with a grim smile at Jack, whilst energetic Eleanor rearranged the luggage inside), when there came a second check.

"Have you got a pin?" Jack asked me.

"I'll see," said I; "what for?"

"To touch up Neddy with. We're going home a rattler."

But on my earnestly remonstrating against the pin, Jack contented himself with pointing a stick, which he assured me would "hurt much more."

"Now, cabby!" he cried, "keep your crawler back till we're well away. You'd better let us go first, or we might pass you on the road, and hurt the feelings of that spirited beast of yours. Do you like going fast, Margery?"

"As fast as you like," said I.

I knew nothing whatever of horses and donkeys, or of what their poor legs could bear; but I very much liked passing swiftly through the air. I do not think Neddy suffered, however, though we went back at a pace marvellously different from that at which we came. We were very light weights, and Master Neddy was an overfed, underworked gentleman, with the acutest discrimination as to his drivers. Jack's voice was quite enough; the stick was superfluous. When we came to the top of the steep hill leading down to the village, Jack asked me, "Shall we go down a rattler?"

"Oh, do!" said I.

"Hold on to the hat-box, then, and don't tumble out."

Down we went. The carriage swayed from side to side; I sat with my arms tightly clasped round the hat-box, and felt as if I were flying straight down on to the church-tower. It was delightful, but I noticed that Jack did not speak till we reached the foot of the hill. Then he said, "Well, that's a blessing! I never thought we should get safe to the bottom."

"Then why did you drive so fast?" I inquired.

"My dear Margery, there's no drag on this carriage; and when I'd once given Neddy his head he couldn't stop himself, no more could I. But he's a plucky, sure-footed little beast; and I shall walk up this hill out of respect for him."

I resolved to do the same, and clambered out, leaving the hat-box on the seat. I went up to Jack, who was patting Neddy's neck, on which he stuck out his right arm, and said, "Link!"

"What?" said I.

"Link," said Jack; and as he stuck out his elbow again in an unmistakable fashion, I took his arm.

"We call that linking, in these parts," said Jack. "Good-evening, Mrs. Loxley. Good-evening, Peter. Thank you, thank you. I'm very glad to get home too—I should think not!" These sentences were replies to the warm greetings Jack received from the cottage-doors; the last to the remark, "You don't find a many places to beat t'ould one, sir, I expect!"

"I'm very popular in the village," said my eccentric companion, with a sigh, as we turned into the drive. "Though I say it that shouldn't, you think? Well! *Ita vita. Such is life's half circle.* Do you know Leadbetter? That's the way he construed it."

"I know you all talk in riddles," said I.

"Well, never mind; you'll know Leadbetter, and all the old books in the house by and by. Plenty of 'em, aren't there? The governor had a curate once, when his throat was bad. *He* said it was an Entertaining Library of Useless Knowledge. I've brought home one more volume to add to it. Second prize for chemistry. Only three fellows went in for it; which you needn't allude to at head-quarters;" and he sighed again.

As we passed slowly under the shadow of the heavy foliage, Jack, like Eleanor, put up his left arm to drag down a bunch of roses. They were further advanced now, and the shower of rose-leaves fell thickly like snowflakes over us—over Jack and me, and Neddy and the carriage, with the hat-box on the driving seat. We must have looked very queer, I think, as we came up out of the overshadowed road, like dwarfs out of a fairy tale, covered with flowers, and leading our carriage with its odd occupant inside.

Keziah, who had been counting the days to the holidays, ran down first to meet us, beaming with pleasure; though when Jack, in the futile attempt to play leap-frog with her against her will, damaged her cap, and clung to her neck till I thought she would have been throttled, she indignantly declared that, "Now the young gentlemen was home there was an end of peace for everybody, choose who they might be."

CHAPTER XXIII.

I CORRESPOND WITH THE MAJOR—MY COLLECTION—OCCUPATIONS—MADAME AGAIN—FÊTE DE VILLAGE—THE BRITISH HOORAY.

I wrote to my old friends and relatives, with a full account of my new home. Rather a comically-expressed account too, I fancy, from the bits Uncle Buller used to quote in after years. I got charming letters from him, piquant with his dry humour, and full of affection. Matilda generally added a note also; and Aunt Theresa always sent love and kisses in abundance, to atone for being too busy to write by that post.

The fonder I grew of the Arkwrights, the better I seemed to love and understand Uncle Buller. Apart as we were, we had now a dozen interests in common—threads of those intellectual ties over which the changes and chances of this mortal life have so little power.

My sympathy was real, as well as ready, when the Major discovered a new insect, almost invisible by the naked eye, which thenceforward bore the terrible specific name of *Bulleriana*, suggesting a creature certainly not less than a rhinoceros, and surrounding the Major's name with something of the halo of immortality. He was equally glad to hear of Jack's beetles and of my fresh-water shells. I had taken to the latter as being "the only things not yet collected by somebody or other in the house;" and I became so infatuated in the pursuit that I used to get up at four o'clock in the morning to search the damp places and water-herbage by the river, it being emphatically "the early bird who catches" snails. After his great discovery, the Major constantly asked if I had found a specimen of *Helix Vandaleuriana* yet. It was a joke between us—that new shell that I was to discover!

I have an old letter open by me now, in which, writing of the Arkwrights, he says, "Your dear father's daughter could have no better home." And, as I read, my father's last hours come back before me, and I hear the poor faint voice whispering, "You've got the papers, Buller? Arkwright will be kind about it, I'm sure." And, "It's all dark now." And with tears I wonder if he—with whom it is all light now—knows how well his true friends have dealt by me, and how happy I am.

To be busy is certainly half-way to being happy. And yet it is not so with every kind of labour. Some occupations, however, do seem of themselves to be peace-bringing; I mean, to be so independent of the great good of being occupied at all. Gardening, sketching, and natural history pursuits, for instance. Is it partly because one follows them in the open air, in great measure?—fresh air, that mysteriously mighty power for good! Anodyne, as well as tonic; dispeller of fever when other remedies are powerless; and the best accredited recipe for long life. Only partly, I think.

One secret of the happiness of some occupations is, perhaps, that they lift one away from petty cares and petty spites, without trying the brain or strength unduly, as some other kinds of mental labour must do. And how delightful is fellowship in such interests! What rivalries without bitterness; what gossip without scandal; what gifts and exchanges; what common interests and mutual sympathy!

In such happy business the holidays went by. Then the question arose, Were we to go back to school? Very earnestly we hoped not; and I think the Arkwrights soon resolved not to send Eleanor away again. As to me, the case was different. Mr. Arkwright felt that he must do what was best for my education: and he wrote to consult with Major Buller.

Fortunately for Eleanor and me, the Major was now as much prejudiced against girls' schools as he had been against governesses; and as masters were to be had at the nearest town, a home education was decided upon. It met with the approval of such of my relatives as were consulted—my great-grandmother especially—and it certainly met with mine.

Eleanor and I were very anxious to show that idleness was not our object in avoiding Bush House. The one of my diaries that escaped burning has, on the fly-leaf, one of the many "lesson plans" we made for ourselves.

We used to get up at six o'clock, and work before breakfast. Certain morning headaches, to which at this time I became subject, led to a serious difference of opinion between me and Mrs. Arkwright; she forbidding me to get up, and I holding myself to be much aggrieved, and imputing the headaches to anything rather than what Keziah briefly termed "book-larning upon an empty stomach." The matter was compromised, thanks to Keziah, by that good creature's offering to bring me new milk and bread-and-butter every morning before I began to work. She really brought it before I dressed, and my headaches vanished.

Though we did not wish to go back to Bush House, we were not quite unmindful of our friends there. Eleanor wrote to thank Madame for the flowers, and received a long and enthusiastic letter in reply—in French, of course, and pointing out one or two blunders in Eleanor's letter, which was in French also. She begged Eleanor to continue to correspond with her, for the improvement of her "composition."

Poor Madame! She was indeed an indefatigable teacher, and had a real ambition for the success of her pupils, which, in the drudgery of her life, was almost grand.

Strange to say, she once came to the Vicarage. It was during the summer succeeding that in which I came to live with the Arkwrights. She had been in the habit of spending the holidays with a family in the country, where, I believe, she gave some instruction in French and music in return for her expenses. That summer she was out of health, and thinking herself unable to fulfil her part of the bargain, she would not go. After severe struggles with her sensitive scruples, she was persuaded to come to us instead, on the distinct condition that she was to do nothing in the way of "lessons," but talk French with us.

To persuade her to accept any payment for her services was the subject of another long struggle. The thriftiest of women in her personal expenditure, and needing money sorely, Madame was not grasping. Indeed, her scruples on this subject were troublesome. She was for ever pursuing us, book in hand, and with a sun-veil and umbrella to shield her complexion, into the garden or the hayfield, imploring us to come in out of the wind and sun, and do "a little of dictation—of composition," or even to permit her to hear us play that duet from the 'Semiramide,' of which the time had seemed to her on the last occasion far from perfect.

Her despair when Mrs. Arkwright supported our refusals was comical, and she was only pacified at last by having the "scrap-bag" of odds and ends of net, muslin, lace, and embroidery handed over to her, from which she made us set after set of dainty collars and sleeves in various "modes," sitting well under the shade of the trees, on a camp-stool, with a camphor-bag to keep away insects, and in bodily fear of the dogs.

Poor Madame! I thought she would have had a fit on the first night of her arrival, when the customary civility was paid of offering her a dog to sleep on her bed. She never got really accustomed to them, and they never seemed quite to understand her. To the end of her stay they snuffed at her black skirts suspiciously, as if she were still more or less of an enigma to them. Madame was markedly civil to them, and even addressed them from time to time as "bons enfants," in imitation of our phrase "dear boys"; but more frequently, in watching the terms on which they lived with the family, she would throw up her little brown hands and exclaim, "*Ménage extraordinaire!*"

I am sure she thought us a strange household in more ways than one, but I think she grew fond of us. For Eleanor she had always had a liking; about Eleanor's mother she became rhapsodical.

"How good!" so she cried to me, "and how truthful—how altogether truthful! What talents also, my faith! Miss Arkwright has had great advantages. A mother extraordinary!"

Mrs. Arkwright had many discussions with Madame on political subjects, and also on the education of girls. On the latter their views were so essentially different, that the discussion was apt to wax hot. Madame came at last to allow that for English girls Madame Arkwright's views might be just, but *pour les filles françaises*—she held to her own opinions.

With the boys she got on very well. At first they laughed at her; then Clement became polite, and even learned to speak French with her after a fashion. Jack was not only ignorant of French, but his English was so mixed with school-boy idioms, that Madame and he seldom got through a conversation without wonderful complications, from which, however, Jack's expressive countenance and ready wit generally delivered them in the long run. I do not know whether, on the whole, Madame did not like Mr. Arkwright best of all. *Le bon pasteur*, as she styled him.

"The Furrin Lady," as she was called in the village, was very fond of looking into the cottages, and studying the ways of the country generally.

I never shall forget the occurrence of the yearly village fair or feast during her visit: her anxiety to be present—her remarkable costume on the occasion—and the strong conviction borne in upon Eleanor and me that the Fat Lady in the centre booth was quite a secondary attraction to the Furrin Lady between us, with the raw lads and stolid farmers who had come down from the hills, with their wise sheep-dogs at their heels. If they stared at her, however, Madame was not unobservant of them, and the critical power was on her side.

"These men and their dogs seem to me alike," said she. "Both of them—they stare so much and say so little. But the looks of the dogs are altogether the more *spirituels*," she added.

I should not like to record all that she said on the subject of our village feast. It was not complimentary, and to some extent the bitter general observations on our national amusements into which her disappointment betrayed her were justified by facts. But it was not our fault that, in translating village feast into *fête de village*, she had allowed her imagination to mislead her with false hopes. She had expected a maypole, a dance of peasants, gay dresses, smiling faces, songs, fruit, coffee, flowers, and tasteful but cheap wares of small kinds in picturesque booths. She had adorned herself, and Eleanor and me, with collars and cuffs of elaborate make and exquisite "get-up" by her own hands. She wore a pale pink and a dead scarlet geranium, together with a spray of wistaria leaf, in admirable taste, on her dark dress.

Her hat was marvellous; her gloves were perfect. She had a few shillings in her pocket to purchase souvenirs for the household; her face beamed in anticipation of a day of simple, sociable, uncostly pleasure, such as we English are so lamentably ignorant of. But I think the only English thing she had prepared herself to expect was what she called "The Briteesh hooray."

Dirt, clamour, oyster-shells, ginger-beer bottles, stolid curiosity, beery satisfaction, careworn stall-keepers with babies-in-arms and strange trust about their wares and honesty over change; giddy-go-rounds, photograph booths, marionettes, the fat woman, the double-headed monstrosity, and the teeming beer-houses——

Poor Madame! The contrast was terrible. She would not enter a booth. She turned homewards in a rage of vexation, and shut herself up in her bedroom (I suspect with tears of annoyance and disappointment), whilst Eleanor and I went back into the feast, and were photographed with dear boys and Clement.

Clement was getting towards an age when clever youngsters are not unapt to exercise their talents in depreciating home surroundings. He said that it was no wonder that Madame was disgusted, and scolded us for taking her into the feast. Jack took quite a different view of the matter.

"The feast's very good fun in its way," said he; "and Madame only wants *tackling*. I'll tackle her."

"Nonsense!" said Clement.

"I bet you a shilling I take her through every mortal thing this afternoon," said Jack.

"You've cheek enough," retorted his elder brother.

But after luncheon, when Madame was again in her room, Jack came to me with a nosegay he had gathered, to beg me to arrange it properly, and put a paper frill round it. With some grass and fern-leaves, I made a tasteful bouquet, and added a frill, to Jack's entire satisfaction. He took it up-stairs, and we heard him knock at Madame's door. After a pause ("I'm sure she's crying again!" said Eleanor) Madame came out, and a warm discussion began between them, of which we only heard fragments. Madame's voice, as the shrillest, was most audible, and it rose into distinctness as she exclaimed, "Anything sŏh dirrty, sŏh meean, sŏh folgaire, I nevaire saw."

Again the discussion proceeded, and we only caught a few of Jack's arguments about "customs of the country," "for the fun of it," etc.

"Fun?" said Madame.

“For a joke,” said Jack.

“*Ah, c’est vrai*, for the choke,” she said.

“And *avec moi*,” Jack continued. “There’s French for you, Madame! Come along!”

Madame laughed. “She’ll

go,” said Eleanor.

“*Eh bien!*” Madame cried gaily. “For the choke. *Avec vous, Monsieur Jack.* Ha! ha! *Allons!* Come along!”

“Link, Madame,” said Jack, as they came down-stairs, Madame smarter than ever, and bouquet in hand.

“Mais *link*? What is this?” said she.

“Take my arm,” said Jack. “I’ll treat you to everything.”

“Mais *treat*? What is that?” said Madame, whose beaming good-humour only expanded the more when Jack explained that it was a pecuniary attention shown by rustic swains to their “young women.”

As Clement came into the hall he met Madame hanging on Jack’s arm, and absolutely radiant.

“You’re not going into that beastly place again?” said he.

“For the choke, Monsieur Clement. *Ah, oui!* And with Monsieur Jack.”

“You may as well come, Clem,” said Eleanor, and we followed, laughing.

Madame had now no time for discontent. Jack held her fast. He gave her gingerbread at one stall, and gingerbeer at another, and cracked nuts for her all along. He vowed that the oyster-shells were flowers, and the empty bottles bouquet-holders, and offered to buy her a pair of spectacles to see matters more clearly with.

“Couleur de rose?” laughed Madame.

We went in a body to the marionettes, and Madame screamed as we climbed the inclined plane to enter, and scrambled down the frail scaffolding to the “reserved seats.” These cost twopence a head, and were “reserved” for us alone. The dolls were really cleverly managed. They performed the closing scenes of a pantomime. The policeman came to pieces when clown and harlequin pulled at him. People threw their heads at each other, and shook their arms off. The transformation scene was really pretty, and it only added to the joke that the dirty old proprietor burned the red light under our very noses, amid a storm of chaff from Jack.

From the marionettes we went to the fat woman. A loathsome sight, which turned me sick; but, for some inexplicable reason, seemed highly to gratify Madame. She and Jack came out in fits of laughter, and he said, "Now for the two-headed monstrosity. It'll just suit you, Madame!"

At the door, Madame paused. "Mais, ce n'est pas pour des petites filles," she said, glancing at Eleanor and me.

"*Feel?*" said Jack, who was struggling through the crowd, which was dense here. "It feels nothing. It's in a bottle. Come along!"

"All right, Madame," said Eleanor, smiling. "We'll wait for you outside."

We next proceeded to the photographer's, where Jack and Madame were photographed together with Pincher.

By Madame's desire she was now led to the "bazaar," where she bought a collar for Pincher, two charming china boxes, in the shape of dogs' heads, for Eleanor and her mother, a fan for me, a walking-stick for Monsieur le Pasteur, and some fishing-floats for Clement. By this time some children had gathered round us. The children of the district were especially handsome, and Madame was much smitten by their rosy cheeks and many-shaded flaxen hair.

"Ah!" she sighed, "I must make some little presents to the children;" and she looked anxiously over the stalls.

"Violin, one and six," said the saleswoman. "Nice work-box for a little girl, half-a-crown."

"Half a fiddlestick," said Jack promptly. "What have you got for a halfpenny?"

"Them's halfpenny balls, whips, and dolls. Them churns and mugs is a halfpenny; and so's the little tin plates. Them's the halfpenny monkeys on sticks."

"Now, Madame," said Jack, "put that half-crown back, and give me a shilling. Twenty-two, twenty-three, twenty-four. There are your presents; and now for the children!"

Madame showed a decided disposition to reward personal beauty, which Jack overruled at once.

"The prettiest? I see myself letting you! Church Sunday scholars is my tip; and I shall put them through the Catechism test. Look here, young un, what's your name? Who gave you this name?"

"Ma godfeythers and godmoothers," the young urchin began.

"That'll do," said Jack. "Take your whip, and be thankful. Now, my little lass, who gave you this name?"

"Me godfeythers——"

"All right. Take your doll, and drop a curtsy; and mind you don't take the curtsy, and drop your doll. Now, my boy, tell me how many there be?"

"Ten."

"Which be they? I mean, take your monkey, and make your bow. Next child, come up."

Clem, Eleanor, and I kept back the crowd as well as we could; but children pressed in on all sides. Clem brought a shilling out of his pocket, and handed it over to Jack.

"You've won your bet, old man," he said.

"You're a good fellow, Clem. I say, lay it out among the halfpenny lot—will you?—and then give them to Madame. Keep your eye open for Dissenters, and send the Church children first."

The forty-eight halfpennyworths proved to be sufficient for all, however, though the orthodoxy of one or two seemed doubtful.

Madame was tired; but the position had pleased her, and she gave away the toys with a charming grace. We were leaving the fair when some small urchins, who had either got or hoped to get presents, and were (I suspected) partly impelled also by a sense of the striking nature of Madame's appearance, set up a lusty cheer.

Madame paused. Her eyes brightened; her thin lips parted with a smile. In a voice of intense satisfaction, she murmured:

"It is the Briteesh hooray!"

CHAPTER XXIV.

WE AND THE BOYS—WE AND THE BOYS AND OUR FADS—THE LAMP OF ZEAL—CLEMENT ON UNREALITY—JACK'S OINTMENT.

Our life on the moors was, I suppose, monotonous. I do not think we ever found it dull; but it was not broken, as a rule, by striking incidents.

The coming and going of the boys were our chief events. We packed for them when they went away. We wrote long letters to them, and received brief but pithy replies. We spoke on their behalf when they wanted clothes or pocket-money. We knew exactly how to bring the news of good marks in school and increased subscriptions to cricket to bear in effective combination upon the parental mind, and were amply rewarded by half a sheet, acknowledging the receipt of a ten-shilling piece in a match-box (the Arkwrights had a strange habit of sending coin of the realm by post, done up like botanical specimens), with brief directions as to the care of garden or collection, and perhaps a rude outline of the head-master's nose—"In a great hurry, from your loving and grateful Bro."

We kept their gardens tidy, preserved their collections from dust, damp, and Keziah, and knitted socks for them. I learned to knit, of course. Every woman knits in that village of stone. And "between lights" Eleanor and I plied our needles on the boys' behalf, and counted the days to the holidays.

We had fresh "fads" every holidays. Many of our plans were ambitious enough, and the results would, no doubt, have been great had they been fully carried out. But Midsummer holidays, though long, are limited in length.

Once we made ourselves into a Field Naturalists' Club. We girls gave up our "spare dress wardrobe" for a museum. We subdivided the shelves, and proposed to make a perfect collection of the flora and entomology of the neighbourhood. Eleanor and I really did continue to add specimens whilst the boys were at school; but they came home at Christmas devoted, body and soul, to the drama. We were soon converted to the new fad. The wardrobe became a side-scene in our theatre, and Eleanor and Clement laboured day and night with papers of powdered paint, and kettles of hot size, in converting canvas into scenery. "Theatricals" promised to be a lasting fancy; but the next holidays were in fine weather, and we made the drop-curtain into a tent.

When the boys were at school, Eleanor and I were fully occupied. We took a good deal of pains with our room: half of it was mine now. I had my knick-knack table as well as Eleanor, my own books and pictures, my own photographs of the boys and of the dear boys, my own pot plants, and my own dog—a pug, given to me by Jack, and named "Saucebox." In Jack's absence, Pincher also looked on me as his mistress.

Like most other conscientious girls, we had rules and regulations of our own devising: private codes, generally kept in cipher, for our own personal self-discipline, and laws common to us both for the employment of our time in joint duties—lessons, parish work, and so forth. I think we made rather too many rules, and that we re-made them too often. I make fewer now, and easier ones, and let them much more alone. I wonder if I really keep them better? But if not, may God, I pray Him, send me back the restless zeal, the hunger and thirst after righteousness, which He gives in early youth! It is so easy to become more thick-skinned in conscience, more tolerant of evil, more hopeless of good, more careful of one's own comfort and one's own property, more self-satisfied in leaving high aims and great deeds to enthusiasts, and then to believe that one is growing older and wiser. And yet those high examples, those good works, those great triumphs over evil, which single hands effect sometimes, we are all grateful for, when they are done, whatever we may have said of the doing. But we speak of saints and enthusiasts for good, as if some special gifts were made to them in middle age which are withheld from other men. Is it not rather that some few souls keep alive the lamp of zeal and high desire which God lights for most of us while life is young?

Eleanor and I worked at our lessons by ourselves. We always had her mother to "fall back upon," as we said. When we took up the study of Italian in order to be able to read Dante—moved thereto by the attractions of the long volume of Flaxman's illustrations of the 'Divina Commedia'—we had to "fall back" a good deal on Mrs. Arkwright's scholarship. And this in spite of all the helps the library afforded us, the best of dictionaries, English "cribs," and about six of those elaborate commentaries upon the poem, of which Italians have been so prolific.

During the winter the study of languages was commonly uppermost; in summer sketching was more favoured.

I do think sketching brings one a larger amount of pleasure than almost any other occupation. And like "collecting," it is a very sociable pursuit when one has fellow-sketchers as well as fellow-naturalists. And this, I must confess, is a merit in my eyes, I being of a sociable disposition! Eleanor could live alone, I think, and be happy; but I depend largely on my fellow-creatures.

Jack and I were talking rather sentimentally the other day about "old times," and I said:

"How jolly it was, that summer we used to sketch so much—all four of us together!"

And Jack, who was rubbing some new stuff of his own compounding into his fishing-boots, replied:

"Awfully. I vote we take to it again when the weather's warmer."

But Jack is so sympathetic, he will agree with anything one says. Indeed, I am sure that he feels what one feels—for the time, at any rate.

Clement is very different. He always disputes and often snubs what one says; partly, I am sure, from a love of truth—a genuine desire to keep himself and everybody else from talking in an unreal way, and from repeating common ideas without thinking them out at first hand; and partly, too, from what Keziah calls the "contradictiousness" of his temper. He was in the room when Jack and I were talking, but he was not talking with us. He was reading for his examination.

All the Arkwrights can work through noise and in company, having considerable powers of mental abstraction. I think they even sometimes combine attention to their own work with an occasional skimming of the topics current in the room as well.

Some outlying feeler of Clement's brain caught my remark and Jack's reply.

"My dear Margery," said he, "you are at heart one of the most unaffected people I know. Pray be equally genuine with your head, and do not encourage Jack in his slipshod habits of thought and conversation by——"

"Slipshod!" interrupted Jack, holding his left arm out at full length before him, the hand of which was shod with a fishing-boot. "Slipshod! They fit as close as your convictions, and would be as stiff and inexorable as logic if I didn't soften them with this newly-invented and about-to-be-patented ointment by the warmth of a cheerful fire and Margery's beaming countenance."

Clement had been reading during this sentence. Then he lifted his head, and said pointedly:

"What I was going to advise *you*, Margery, is never to get into the habit of adopting sentiments till you are quite sure you really mean them. It is by the painful experience of my own folly that I know what trouble it gives one afterwards. If ever the time comes when you want to know your real opinion on any subject, the process of getting rid of ideas you have adopted without meaning them will not be an easy one."

I am not as intellectual as the Arkwrights. I can always see through Jack's jokes, but I am sometimes left far behind when Eleanor or Clement "take flight," as Jack calls it, on serious subjects. I really did not follow Clement on this occasion.

With some hesitation I said:

"I don't know that I quite understand."

"I'm sure you don't," said Jack. "I have feared for some time that your hair was getting too thick for the finer ideas of this household to penetrate to your brain. Allow me to apply a little of this ointment to the parting, which in your case is more definite than with Eleanor; and as our lightest actions should proceed from principles, I may mention that the principle on which I propose to apply the Leather-softener to your scalp is that on which the blacksmith's wife gave your cholera medicine to the second girl, when she began with rheumatic fever—'it did such a deal of good to our William.' Now, this unguent has done 'a deal of good' to the leather of my boots. Why should it not successfully lubricate the skin of your skull?"

Only the dread of "a row" between Jack and Clem enabled me to keep anything like gravity.

"Don't talk nonsense, Jack!" said I, as severely as I could. (I fear that, like the rest of the world, I snubbed Jack rather than Clement, because his temper was sweeter, and less likely to resent it.) "Clement, I'm very stupid, but I don't quite see how what *you* said applies to what *I* said."

"You said, 'How happy we were, that summer we went sketching!' or words to that effect. It's just like a man's writing about the careless happiness of childhood, when he either forgets, or refuses to advert to, the toothache, the measles, learning his letters, the heat of the night-nursery, not being allowed to sit down in the yard whilst his knickerbockers were new, going to bed at eight o'clock, and having a lie on his conscience. I have striven for more accurate habits of thought, and I remember distinctly that you cried over more than one of your sketches."

"I got into the 'Household Album' with mine, however," said Jack; "and I defy an A.R.A. to have had more difficulty in securing his position."

"I'm afraid your appearance in the *Phycological Quarterly* was better deserved," said Mrs. Arkwright, without removing her eye from the microscope she was using at a table just opposite to Clem's.

But this demands explanation, and I must go back to the time of which Jack and I spoke—when we used to go sketching together.

CHAPTER XXV.

THE "HOUSEHOLD ALBUM"—SKETCHING UNDER DIFFICULTIES—A NEW SPECIES?—JACK'S BARGAIN—THEORIES.

Out of motherly affection, and also because their early attempts at drawing were very clever, Mrs. Arkwright had, years before, begun a scrapbook, or "Household Album," as it was called, into which she pasted such of her children's original drawings as were held good enough for the honour; the age of the artist being taken into account.

Jack's gift in this line was not as great as that of Clement or Eleanor, but this was not the only reason why no drawing of his appeared in the scrapbook. Mrs. Arkwright demanded more evidence of pains and industry than Jack was wont to bestow on his sketches or designs. He resented his exclusion, and made many efforts to induce his mother to accept his hasty productions; but it was not till the summer to which I alluded that Jack took his place in the "Household Album."

It was during a long drive, in which we were exhibiting the country to some friends, that Eleanor and I chose the place of that particular sketching expedition. The views it furnished had the first, and almost the only, quality demanded by young and tyro sketchers—they were very pretty.

There was some variety, too, to justify our choice. From the sandy road, where a heathery bank afforded the convenience of seats, we could look down into a valley with a winding stream, whose banks rose into hillsides which lost themselves in finely-coloured mountains of moorland.

Farther on, a scramble on foot over walls and gates had led us into a wooded gorge fringed with ferns, where a group of trees of particularly graceful form roused Eleanor's admiration.

"What a lovely view!" had burst from the lips of our friends at every quarter of a mile; for they were of that (to me) trying order of carriage companions who talk about the scenery as you go, as a point of politeness.

But the views *were* beautiful—"Sketches everywhere!" we cried.

"There's nothing to make a sketch *of* round the Vicarage," we added. "We've done the church, with the Deadmanstone Hills behind it, and without the Deadmanstone Hills behind it, till we are sick of the subject."

So, the weather being fine, and even hot, we provided ourselves with luncheon and sketching materials, and made an expedition to the point we had selected.

We were tired by the time we reached it. This does not necessarily damp one's sketching ardour, but it is unfavourable to accuracy of outline, and especially so to purity of colouring. However, we did not hesitate. Eleanor went down to her study of birch-trees in the gorge, Clement climbed up the bank to get the most extended view of the Ewden Valley; I contented myself with sitting by the roadside in front of the same view, and Jack stayed with me.

He had come with us. Not that he often went out sketching, but our descriptions of the beauty of the scenery had roused him to make another attempt for the "Household Album." Seldom lastingly provided, for his own part, with apparatus of any kind, Jack had a genius for purveying all that he required in an emergency. On this occasion he had borrowed Mrs. Arkwright's paint-box (without leave), and was by no means ill supplied with pencils and brushes which certainly were not his own. He had hastily stripped a couple of sheets from my block whilst I was dressing, and with these materials he seated himself on that side of me which enabled him to dip into my water-pot, and began to paint.

Not half-way through my outline, I was just beginning to realize the complexities of a bird's-eye view with your middle distance in a valley, and your foreground sloping steeply upwards to your feet, when Jack, washing out a large, dyed sable sky-brush in my pot, with an amount of splashing that savoured of triumph, said:

"*That's* done!"

I paused in a vigorous mental effort to put aside my *knowledge* of the relative sizes of objects, and to *see* that a top stone of my foreground wall covered three fields, the river, and half the river's bank beyond.

"*Done?*" I exclaimed. Jack put his brush into his mouth, in defiance of all rules, and deliberately sucked it dry. Then he waved his sketch before my eyes.

"The effect's rather good," I confessed, "but oh, Jack, it's out of all proportion! That gate really looks as big as the whole valley and the hills beyond. The top of the gate-post ought to be up in the sky."

"It would look beastly ugly if it was," replied he complacently.

"You've got a very good tint for those hills; but the foreground is mere scrambling. Oh, Jack, do finish it a little more! You would draw so nicely if you had any patience."

"How imperfectly you understand my character," said Jack, packing up his traps. "I would sit on a monument and smile at grief with any one, this very day, if the monument were in a grove, or even if I had an umbrella to smile under. To sit unsheltered under this roasting sun, and make myself giddy by gauging proportions with a pencil at the end of my nose, or smudging my mistakes with melting india-rubber, is quite another matter. I'm off to Eleanor. I've got another sheet of paper, and I think trees are rather in my line."

"I *thought* my block looked smaller," said I, rapidly comparing Jack's paper and my own, with a feeling for size developed by my labours.

"Has she got a water-pot?" asked Jack.

"She is sure to have," said I pointedly. "She always takes her own materials with her."

"How fortunate for those who do not!" said Jack. "Now, Margery dear, don't look sulky. I knew you wouldn't grudge me a bit of paper to get into the 'Household Album' with. Come down into the ravine. You're as white as a blank sheet of Whatman's hot-pressed water-colour paper!"

The increasing heat was really beginning to overpower me, but I refused to leave my sketch. Jack pinned a large white pocket-handkerchief to my shoulders—"to keep the sun from the spine"—and departed to the ravine.

By midday my outline was in. One is no good judge of one's own work, but I think, on the whole, that it was a success.

It is always refreshing to complete a stage of anything. I began to feel less hot and tired, as I passed a wash of clean water over my outline, and laying it in the sun to dry, got out my colours and brushes.

As I did so, one of the little gusts of wind which had been an unpleasant feature of this very fine day, and which, threatening a change of weather, made us anxious to finish our sketches at a sitting, came down the sandy road. In an instant the damp surface of my block looked rough enough to strike matches on. But impatience is not my besetting sin, and I had endured these little catastrophes before. I waited for the block to dry before I brushed off the sand. I also waited till the little beetle, who had crept into my sky, and was impeded in his pace by my first wash, walked slowly down through all my distances, and quitted the block by the gate in the foreground. This was partly because I did not want to hurt him, and partly because a white cumulus cloud is a bad part of your sketch to kill a black beetle on.

I washed over my paper once more, and holding it on my knee to dry just as much and no more than was desirable, I looked my subject in the face with a view to colour.

A long time passed. I had looked and looked again; I had washed in and washed out; I had realized the difficulty of the subject without flinching, and had tried hard to see and represent the colouring before me, when Clement (having exhausted his water in a similar process) came down the hill behind me, with a surly and sunburnt face, to replenish his bottle at a wayside water-trough.

It was then that, as he said, he found me crying.

"It's not because it's difficult and I'm very stupid," I whimpered. "I don't mind working on and trying to make the best of a thing. And it's not the wind or the sand, though it has got dreadfully into the paints, particularly the Italian Pink; but what makes me hopeless, Clement, is that I don't believe it would look well if I could paint it perfectly. It looked lovely as we were driving home the other evening, but now—— Just look at those fields, Clem; I *know* they're green, but really and truly I *see* them just the same colour as this road, and I don't think there is the difference of a shade between them and that gate-post. What shall I do?"

A tear fell out of my eyelashes and dropped on to my river. Clement took the sketch from me, and dried up the tear with a bit of blotting-paper.

Then to my amazement he gave rather a favourable verdict. It comforted me, for Clement never says anything that he does not mean.

"It's not *half* bad, Margery! Wait till you see mine! How did you get the tints of that hillside? You've a very truthful mind, that's one thing, and a very true eye as well. I do admire the way you abstain from filling up with touches that mean nothing."

"Oh, Clement!" cried I, so gratified that I began to feel ready to go on again. "Do you really think I can make anything of it?"

"Nothing more," said Clement. "Don't put another touch. It's unfinished, but no finishing would do any good. We've got an outlandish subject and a bad time of day. But keep it just as it is, and three months hence, on a cool day, you'll be pleased when you look at it."

"Perhaps if I went on a little with the foreground," I suggested; but even as I spoke, I put my hand to my head.

"Go to Eleanor in the ravine, at once," said Clement imperatively. "I'll bring your things. What *did* make us such fools as to come out without umbrellas?"

"We came out in the cool of the morning," said I, as I staggered off;

"besides, it's almost impossible to hold one and paint too."

Once in the ravine, I dropped among the long grass and ferns, and the damp, refreshing coolness of my resting-place was delicious.

Eleanor was not faint, neither had she been crying; but she was not much happier with her sketch than I had been with mine. The jutting group of birch-trees was well chosen, and she had drawn them admirably. But when she came to add the confused background of trees and undergrowth, her very outline had begun to look less satisfactory. When it came to colour—and the midday sun was darting and glittering through the interstices of the trees, without supplying any effects of *chiaroscuro* to a subject already defective in point and contrast—Eleanor was almost in despair.

"Where's Jack?" said I, after condoling with her.

"He tried the birches for ten minutes, and then he went up the stream to look for *algæ*."

At this moment Jack appeared. He came slowly towards us, looking at something in his hand.

"Lend me your magnifying-glass, Eleanor," said he, when he had reached us.

Eleanor unfastened it from her chatelaine, and Jack became absorbed in examining some water-weed in a dock-leaf.

"What is it?" said we.

"It's a new species, I believe. Look, Eleanor!" and he gave her the leaf and the glass with an almost pathetic anxiety of countenance.

My opinion carried no weight in the matter, but Eleanor was nearly as good a naturalist as her mother. And she was inclined to agree with Jack.

"It's too good to be true! But I certainly don't know it. Where did you find it?"

"No, thank you," said Jack derisively. "I mean to keep the habitat to myself for the present. For *a very good reason*. Margery, my child, put that sketch of mine into the pocket of your block. (The paper is much about the size of your own!) It is going into the 'Household Album.'"

We went home earlier than we had intended. Even the perseverance of Eleanor and Clement broke down under their ill-success. Jack was the only well-satisfied one of the party, and, with his usual good-nature, he tried hard to infect me with his cheerfulness.

"I think," said I, looking dolefully at my sketch, "that a good deal of the fault must have been in my eyes. I suspect one can't see colours properly when one is feeling sick and giddy. But the glare of the sun was the worst. I couldn't tell red from green on my palette, so no wonder the fields and everything else looked all the same colour. And yet what provokes one is the feeling that an artist would have made a sketch of it somehow. The view is really beautiful."

"And that is really beautiful," said Eleanor, pointing to the birch group and its background. "And what a mess I have made of it! I wish I'd stuck to pencil. And yet, as you say, an artist would have got a picture out ofit."

"I'll tell you what," said Jack, who was lying face downwards with my picture spread before him, "I believe that any one who knew the dodges, when he saw that everything looked one pale, yellowish, brownish tint with the glare of the sun, would have boldly taken a weak wash of all the drab-looking colours in his box right over everything, picked out a few stones in his foreground wall, dodged in a few shadows and so on, and made a clever sketch of it. And the same with Eleanor's. If he had got his birch-trees half as good as hers, and had then seen what a muddle the trees behind were in, I believe he would only have washed in a little blue and grey behind the birches, 'indicated' (as our old drawing-master at school calls it) a distant stem or two—and there would have been another clever sketch for you!"

"Another clever falsehood, you mean," said Clement hotly, "to ruin people's taste, and encourage idle painters in showy trickery, and make them believe they can improve upon Nature's colouring."

"Nature's colouring varies," said Jack. "Distant trees often *are* blue and grey, though these, just now, are of the rankest green."

Clement replied, Jack responded, Clement retorted, and a fierce art-discussion raged the whole way home.

We were well used to it. Indeed all conversations with us had a tendency to become controversial. Over and above which there was truth in Keziah's saying, "The young gentlemen argle-bargles fit to deave a body's head; and dear knows what it's all about."

Clement finished a vehement and rather didactic confession of his art-faith as we climbed the steep hill to the Vicarage. The keynote of it was that one ought to draw what he sees, exactly as he sees it; and that every subject has a beauty of its own which he ought to perceive if his perception is not "emasculated by an acquired taste for prettinesses."

"I shall be in the 'Household Album' this evening," said Jack, in deliberate tones. "My next ambition is the Society of Painters in Water

Colours. The subject of my first painting is settled. Three grass fields (haymaking over the day before yesterday). A wall in front of the first field, a hedge in front of the second, a wall in front of the third. A gate in the middle of the wall. A spotted pig in the middle of the field. The sun at its meridian; the pig asleep. Motto, 'Whatever is, is beautiful.'"

Eleanor and I (in the interests of peace) hastened to change the subject by ridiculing Jack's complacent conviction that his sketch would be accepted for the "Household Album."

And yet it was.

The fresh-water *alga* Jack had been lucky enough to find was a new species, and threw Mrs. Arkwright and Eleanor into a state of the highest excitement. But all their entreaties failed to persuade Jack to disclose the secret of the habitat.

"Put my sketch into the 'Household Album,' and I'll tell you all about it," said he.

Mrs. Arkwright held out against this for half-an-hour. Then she gave way. Jack's sketch was gummed in (it took up a whole page, being the full size of my block), and he told us all about the water-weed.

It was described and figured in the *Phycological Quarterly*, and received the specific name of *Arkwrightii*, and Jack's double triumph was complete.

We were very glad for his success, but it almost increased the sense of disappointment that our share of the expedition had been so unlucky.

"It seems such a waste," said I, "to have got to such a lovely place with one's drawing things and plenty of time, and to come away without a sketch worth keeping at the end, just because one doesn't know the right way of working."

"I think there's a good deal in what Jack said about your sketch," said Eleanor; "and I think if one looked at the way real artists have treated similar subjects, and then went at it again and tried to do it on a similar principle——"

"If ever we do go there again," Clement interrupted, "but I don't suppose we shall—these holidays. And the way summer after summer slips away is awful. I'm more and more convinced that it's a great mistake to have so many hobbies. No life is long enough for more than one pursuit, and it's ten to one you die in the middle of mastering that. One is sure to die in the early stages of half-a-dozen."

Clement is very apt to develop some odd theory of this kind, and to preach it with a severity that borders on gloom. I never know what to say, even if I disagree with him; but Eleanor takes up the cudgels at once.

"I don't think I agree with you," she said, giving a shove to her soft elastic hair which did not improve the indefiniteness of the parting. "Of course it's unsatisfactory in one way to feel one will never live to finish things, but in another way I think it's a great comfort to feel one can never use them up or outlive them if one lasts on to be a hundred. And though one gets very cross and miserable with failing so over things one works at, I don't know whether one would be so much happier when one was at the top of the tree. I'm not sure that the chief pleasure isn't actually in the working at things —I mean in the drudgery of learning, rather than in the triumph of having learnt."

"There's something in that," said Clement. And it was a great deal for Clement to say.

It does not take much to convert *me* to Eleanor's views of anything. But I do think experience bears out what she said about this matter.

Perhaps that accounts for my having a happy remembrance of old times when we worked at things together, even if we failed and cried over them.

I know that practically, now, I would willingly join the others in going at anything, though I could not promise not to be peevish over my own stupidity sometimes, and if I was very much tired.

I don't think there was anything untrue in my calling the times we went sketching together happy times—in spite of what Clement says.

But he does rule such very straight lines all over life, and I sometimes think one may rule them too straight—even for full truth.

CHAPTER XXVI.

MANNERS AND CUSTOMS—CLIQUE—THE LESSONS OF EXPERIENCE—OUT VISITING—HOUSE-PRIDE—DRESSMAKING.

Eleanor and I were not always at home. We generally went visiting somewhere, at least once a year.

I think it was good for us. Great as were the advantages of the life I now shared over an existence wasted in a petty round of ignoble gossip and social struggle, it had the drawback of being almost too self-sufficing, perhaps—I am not certain—a little too laborious. I do think, but for me, it must, at any rate, have become the latter. I am so much less industrious, energetic, clever and good in every way than Eleanor, for one thing, that my very idleness holds us back; and I think a taste for gaiety (I simply mean being gay, not balls and parties), and for social pleasure, and for pretty things, and graceful "situations" runs in my veins with my French blood, and helps to break the current of our labours.

We led lives of considerable intellectual activity, constant occupation, and engrossing interest. We were apt to "foy" at our work to the extent of grudging meal-times and sleep. Indeed, at one time a habit obtained with us of leaving the table in turn as we finished our respective meals. One member of the family after another would rise, bend his or her head for a silent "grace," and depart to the work in hand. I have known the table gradually deserted in this fashion till Mr. Arkwright was left alone. I remember going back one day into the room, and seeing him so. My entrance partially aroused him from a brown study. (He was at all times very "absent") He rose, said grace aloud for the benefit of the company—which had dispersed—and withdrew to his library. But we abolished this uncivilized custom in conclave, and thenceforth sat our meals out to the end.

So free were we in our isolation upon those Yorkshire moors from the trammels of conventionality (one might almost say, civilization!), that I think we should have come to begrudge the ordinary interchange of the neighbourly courtesies of life, but for occasional lectures from Mrs. Arkwright, and for going out visiting from time to time.

It was not merely that a life of running in and out of other people's houses, and chatting the same bits of news threadbare with one acquaintance after another, as at Riflebury, would have been unendurable by us. The rare arrival of a visitor from some distant country-house to call at the Vicarage was the signal for every one, who could do so with decency, to escape from the unwelcome interruption. But as we grew older, Mrs. Arkwright would not allow this. The boys, indeed, were hard to coerce; they "bolted" still when the door-bell rang; but domestic authority, which is apt to be magnified on "the girls," overruled Eleanor and me for our good, and her mother—who reasoned with us far more than she commanded—convinced us of how much selfishness there was in this, as in all acts of discourtesy.

But what do we not owe to her good counsels? In how many evening talks has she not warned us of the follies, affectations, or troubles to which our lives might specially be liable! Against despising interests that are not our own, or graces which we have chosen to neglect, against the danger of satire, against the love or the fear of being thought singular, and, above all, against the petty pride of clique.

"I do not know which is the worst," I remember her saying, "a religious clique, an intellectual clique, a fashionable clique, a moneyed clique, or a family clique. And I have seen them all."

"Come, Mother," said Eleanor, "you cannot persuade us you would not have more sympathy with the intellectual than the moneyed clique, for instance?"

"I should have warmly declared so myself, at one time," said Mrs. Arkwright, "but I have a vivid remembrance of a man belonging to an artistic clique, to whose house I once went with some friends. My friends were artists also, but their minds were enlarged, instead of being narrowed, by one chief pursuit. Their special art gave them sympathy with all others, as the high cultivation of one virtue is said to bring all the rest in its train. But this man talked the shibboleth of his craft over one's head to other members of his clique with a defiance of good manners arising more from conceit than from ignorance of the ways of society; and with a transparent intention of being overheard and admired which reminded me of the little self-conscious conceits of children before visitors. He was one of a large family with the same peculiarities, joined to a devout admiration of each other. Indeed, they combined the artistic clique and the family clique in equal proportions. From the conversation at their table you would have imagined that there was but one standard of good for poor humanity, that of one 'school' of one art, and absolutely no one who quite came up to it but the brothers, sisters, parents, cousins, or connections by marriage of your host. Now, I honestly assure you that the only other man really like this one that I ever met, was what is called a 'self-made' man in a commercial clique. Money was *his* standard, and he seemed to be as completely unembarrassed as my artist friend by the weight of any other ideas than his own, or by any feeling short of utter satisfaction with himself. Their contempt for the conventionalities of society was about equal. My artist friend had passed a sweeping criticism for my benefit now and then (there could be no conversation where no second opinion was allowed), and it was with perhaps a shade less of condescension—a shade more of friendliness—that my commercial friend once stopped some remarks of mine with the knowing observation, 'Look here, ma'am. Whenever I hear this, that, and the other bragged about a party, what I always say is this, I don't want you to tell me what he *his*, but what he *'as*.'"

Eleanor and I laughed merrily at the anecdote, even if we were not quite converted to Mrs. Arkwright's views. And I must in justice add that every visit which has taken us from home—every fresh experience which has enlarged our knowledge of the world—has confirmed the truth of her sage and practical advice.

If at home we have still inclined to feel it almost a duty to be proud of intellectual tastes, quite a duty to be proud of orthodox opinions, and, at the worst, a very amiable weakness indeed to think that there are no boys like our boys, a wholesome experience of having other people's tastes and views crammed down our throats has modified our ideas in this respect. A strong dose of eulogistic biography of the brothers of a gushing acquaintance made the names of Clem and Jack sacred to our domestic circle for ever; and what I have endured from a mangy, over-fed, ill-tempered Skye-terrier, who is the idol of a lady of our acquaintance, has led me sometimes to wonder if visitors at the Vicarage are ever oppressed by the dear boys.

I'm afraid it is possible—poor dear things!

I have positively heard people say that Saucebox is ugly, though he has eyes like a bull-frog, and his tongue hangs quite six inches out of his mouth, and—in warm weather or before meals—further still! However, I keep him in very good order, and never allow him to be troublesome to people who do not appreciate him. For I have observed that there are people who (having no children of their own) hold very just and severe views about spoiled boys and girls, but who (having dogs of their own) are much less clear-sighted on the subject of spoiled terriers and Pomeranians. And I do not want to be like that —dear as the dear boys are!

Certainly, seeing all sorts of people with all sorts of peculiarities is often a great help towards trying to get rid of one's own objectionable ones. But like the sketching, one sometimes gets into despair about it, and though the process of learning an art may be even pleasanter than to feel one's self a master in it, one cannot say as much for the process of discovering one's follies. I should like to get rid of *them* in a lump.

Eleanor said so one day to her mother, but Mrs. Arkwright said: "We may hate ourselves, as you call it, when we come to realize failings we have not recognized before, and feel that there are probably others which we do not yet see as clearly as other people see them, but this kind of impatience for our perfection is not felt by those who love us, I am sure. It is one's greatest comfort to believe that it is not even felt by God. Just as a mother would not love her child the better for its being turned into a model of perfection by one stroke of magic, but does love it the more dearly every time it tries to be good, so I do hope and believe our Great Father does not wait for us to be good and wise to love us, but loves us, and loves to help us in the very thick of our struggles with folly and sin."

But I am becoming as discursive as ever! What I want to put down is about our going out visiting. There is really nothing much to say about our life at home. It was very happy, but there were no great events in it, and Eleanor says it will not do for us to "go off at a tangent," and describe what happened to the boys at school and college; first, because these biographies are merely to be lives of our own selves, for nobody but us two to read when we are both old maids; and secondly, because if we put down everything we had anything to do with in these ten years, it will be so very long before our biographies are finished. We are very anxious to see them done, partly because we are getting rather tired of them, and Jack is becoming suspicious, and partly because we have got an amateur bookbinding press, and we want to bind them.

Well, as I said, we paid visits to relatives of mine, and to old friends of the Arkwrights. My friends invited Eleanor, and Eleanor's friends invited me. People are very kind; and it was understood that we were happier together.

I was fortunate enough to find myself possessed of some charming cousins living in a cathedral town; and at their house it was a great pleasure to us to visit. The cathedral services gave us great delight; when I think of the expression of Eleanor's face, I may almost say rapture. Then there was a certain church-bookseller's shop in the town, which had manifold attractions for us. Every parochial want that print and paper could supply was there met, with a convenience that bordered on luxury. There was a good store, too, of sacred prints, illuminated texts, and oak frames, from which we carried back sundry additions to the garnishing of our room, besides presents for Jack, who was as fond of such things as we were. Parish matters were, naturally, of perennial interest for us in our Vicarage home; but if ever they became a fad, it was about this period.

But it was to a completely new art that this visit finally led us, which I hardly know how to describe, unless as the art of dressmaking and general ornamentation.

The neighbourhood abounded with pretty clerical and country homes, where my cousins were intimate; each one, so it seemed to Eleanor and me, prettier than the last: sunshiny and homelike, with irregular comfortable furniture, dainty with chintz, or dark with aged oak, each room more tastefully besprinkled than the rest with old china, new books, music, sketches, needlework, and flowers.

"Do you know, Eleanor," said I, when we were dressing for dinner one evening before a toilette-table that had been tastefully adorned for our use by the daughters of the house, "I wonder if Yorkshire women *are* as 'house-proud' as they call themselves? I think our villagers are, in the important points of cleanliness and solid comfort, and of course we are at the Vicarage as to *that*—Keziah keeps us all like copper kettles; but don't you think we might have a little more house-pride about tasteful pretty refinements? It perhaps is rather a waste of time arranging all these vases and baskets of flowers every day, but they are *very* nice to look at, and I think it civilizes one."

"*You're* not to blame," said Eleanor decisively. "You're south-country to the backbone, and French on the top. It is we hard north-country folk, we business people, who neglect to cultivate 'the beautiful.' We're quite wrong. But I think the beautiful is revenged on us," added she with one of her quick, bright looks, "by withdrawing itself. There's nothing comparable for ugliness to the people of a manufacturing town."

My mind was running on certain very ingenious and tasteful methods of hanging nosegays on the wall.

"Those baskets with ferns and flowers in, against the wall, were lovely, weren't they?" said I. "Do you think we shall ever be able to think of such pretty things?"

"We're not fools," said Eleanor briefly. "We shall do it when we set our minds to it. Meantime, we must make notes of whatever strikes us."

"There are plenty of jolly, old-fashioned flowers in the garden at home," said I. It was a polite way of expressing my inward regret that we had no tropical orchids or strange stove-plants. And Eleanor danced round me, and improvised a song beginning:

"There are ferns by Ewden's waters,
And heather on the hill."

From the better adornment of the Vicarage to the better adornment of ourselves was a short stride. Most of the young ladies in these country homes were very prettily dressed. Not *à la* Mrs. Perowne. Not in that milliner's handbook style dear to "Promenades" and places of public resort; but more daintily, and with more attention to the prettiest and most convenient of the prevailing fashions than Eleanor's and my costumes displayed.

The toilettes of one young lady in particular won our admiration; and when we learned that her pretty things were made by herself, an overwhelming ambition seized upon us to learn to do the same.

"Women ought to know about all house matters," said Eleanor, puckering her brow to a gloomy extent. "Dressmaking, cookery, and all that sort of thing; and we know nothing about any of them. I was thinking only last night, in bed, that if I were cast away on a desert island, and had to make a dress out of an old sail, I shouldn't have the ghost of an idea where to begin."

"I should," said I. "I should sew it up like a sack, make three holes for my head and arms, and tie it round my waist with ship's rope. I could manage Robinson Crusoe dresses; it's the civilized ones that will be too much for me, I'm afraid."

"I believe the sail would go twice as far if we could gore it," said Eleanor, laughing. "But there's no waste like the wastefulness of ignorance; and oh, Margery, it's the *gores* I'm afraid of! If skirts were only made the old-fashioned way, like a flannel petticoat! So many pieces all alike—run them together—hem the bottom—gather the top—and there you are, with everything straightforward but the pocket."

To our surprise we found that our new fad was a sore subject with Mrs. Arkwright. She reproached herself bitterly with having given Eleanor so little training in domestic arts. But she had been brought up by a learned uncle, who considered needlework a waste of time, and she knew as little about gores as we did. She had also, unfortunately, known or heard of some excellent mother who had trained nine daughters to such perfection of domestic capabilities that it was boasted that they could never in after-life employ a workwoman or domestic who would know more of her business than her employer. And this good lady was a standing trouble to poor Mrs. Arkwright's conscience.

Her self-reproaches were needless. General training is perhaps quite as good as (if not better than) special, even for special ends. In giving us a higher education, in teaching us to use our eyes, our wits, and our common-sense, she had put all meaner arts within our grasp when need should urge, and opportunity serve.

"Aunt Theresa was always dressmaking," I said to Eleanor; "but I don't remember anything that would help us. I was so young, you know. And when one is young one is so stupid, one really resists information."

I was to have another chance, however, of gleaning hints from Aunt Theresa.

CHAPTER XXVII.

MATILDA—BALL DRESSES AND THE BALL—GORES—MISS LINING—THE 'PARISHIONER'S PENNYWORTH.'

The Bullers came home again. Colonel St. Quentin had retired, and when Major Buller got the regiment, he also left the army and settled in a pleasant neighbourhood in the south of England. As soon as Aunt Theresa was fairly established in her new house she sent for Eleanor and me. There was no idea of my remaining permanently. It was only a visit.

The Major (but he was a colonel now) and his wife were very little changed. The girls, of course, had altered greatly, and so had I. Matilda was a fashionably-dressed young lady, with a slightly frail appearance at times, as if Nature were still revenging the old mismanagement and neglect.

It did not need Aunt Theresa to tell us that she was her father's favourite daughter. But it was no capricious favouritism, I am sure. I believe Colonel Buller to have been one of those people whose hearts have depths of tenderness that are never sounded. The Bush House catastrophe had long ago been swept into the lumber-room of Aunt Theresa's memory, but the tender self-reproach of Matilda's father was still to be seen in all his care and indulgence of her.

"He'll take me anywhere," said Matilda, with affectionate pride. "He even goes shopping with me."

We liked Matilda by far the best of the girls. Partly, no doubt, because she was our old friend, but partly, I think, because intimacy with her father had developed the qualities she inherited from him, and softened others.

To our great satisfaction we discovered that gores were no enigma to Matilda, and she and Aunt Theresa good-naturedly undertook to initiate us into the mysteries of dressmaking.

There was an excellent opportunity. Eleanor was now eighteen, and Matilda seventeen years old. Matilda was to "come out" at a county ball that was to take place whilst we were with the Bullers, and Mrs. Arkwright consented to let Eleanor go also. Hence ball dresses, and hence also our opportunity for learning how to make them. For they were to be made by a dressmaker in the house, and she did not reject our assistance.

The Bullers' drawing-room was divided by folding-doors, and both divisions now overflowed with tarlatan and trimmings; but at every fresh inroad of callers (and they were hardly less frequent than of old) we young ones, and yards of flounces and finery with us, were swept by Aunt Theresa into the back drawing-room, like autumn leaves before a breeze.

The dresses were very successful, and so was the ball. I was so anxious to hear how Eleanor had sped, that I felt quite sure that I could not go to sleep, and that it was a farce to go to bed just when she was beginning to dance. I went, however, at last, and had had half a night's sound sleep before rustling, and chattering, and the light from bed-candles woke me to hear the news.

Matilda was looking pale, and somewhat dishevelled, and a great deal of the costume at which we had laboured was reduced to rags. Eleanor's dress was intact, and she herself looked perfectly fresh, partly because she had resisted, with great difficulty, the extreme length of train then fashionable, and partly from a sort of general compactness which seems a natural gift with some people. Poor Matilda had nearly fainted after one of the dances, and had brought away a violent headache; but she declared that she had enjoyed herself, and would have stayed to relate her adventures, but Colonel Buller would not allow it, and sent her to bed. Eleanor slept with me, so our gossip was unopposed, except by warnings.

I set fire to my hair in the effort to decipher the well-filled ball card, but we put it out, and the candle also, and chatted in bed.

"You must have danced every dance," I said, admiringly.

"We sat out one or two that are down," said Eleanor; "and No. 21 was supper, but I danced all the rest."

"There was one man you danced several times with," I said, "but I couldn't make out his name. It looks as if it began with a G."

"Oh, it's not his real name," said Eleanor. "It's the one he says you used to call him by. One reason why I liked him, Margery dear, was because he said he had been so fond of you. You were such a dear little thing, he said. I told him the locket and chain were in good preservation."

"Was it Mr. George?" I cried, with so much energy that Aunt Theresa (who slept next door) heard us, and knocked on the wall to bid us go to sleep.

"We're just going to," Eleanor shouted, and added in lower tones, to me, "Yes, it was Captain Abercrombie. Colonel Buller introduced him to me. He is so nice, and so delightfully fond of dogs and of you, Margery."

"Shall I see him?" I asked. "I should like to see him again. He was very good to me when I was little."

"Oh yes," said Eleanor. "It was curious his being in the neighbourhood; for the 202nd is in Dublin, you know. And, Margery, he says he has an uncle in Yorkshire. He——"

"Girls! girls!" cried Aunt Theresa; and we went to sleep.

Soon after we returned from our visit to the Bullers, Eleanor and I resolved to prove the benefit we had reaped from Aunt Theresa's instructions by making ourselves some dresses of an inexpensive stuff that we bought for the purpose.

How well I remember the pattern! A flowering creeper, which followed a light stem upwards through yard after yard of the material. We had picked to pieces certain old bodies which fitted us fairly, and our first work was to lay these patterns upon the new stuff, with weights on them, and so to cut out our new bodies as easily as Matilda (whose directions we were following) had prophesied that we should. When these and the sleeves were accomplished (and they looked most business-like), we began upon the skirts. We cut the back and the front breadths, and duly "sloped" the latter. Then came the gores. We folded the breadths into three parts; we took a third at one end, and two-thirds at the other, and folded the slope accordingly. It became quite exciting.

"Who would have thought it was so easy?" said I.

Eleanor was almost prone upon the table, cutting the gores with large scissors which made a thoroughly sempstress-like squeak.

"The higher education fades from my view with every snip," she said, laughing. "Upon my word, Margery, I begin to believe this sort of thing *is* our vocation. It is great fun, and there is absolutely no brain wear and tear."

The gores were parted as she spoke, and (to do us justice) were exactly the shape of the tarlatan ones Aunt Theresa had cut. But when we came to put them together, they wouldn't fit without turning one of them the wrong side out. Eleanor had boasted too soon. We got headaches and backaches with stooping and puzzling. We cut up all our stuff, but the gores remained obstinate. By no ingenuity could we combine them so as to be at once in proper order, the right side out, and the right side (of the pattern) up. I really think we cried over them with weariness and disappointment.

"Algebra's a trifle to it," was poor Eleanor's conclusion.

I went out to clear my brain by a walk, and happening, as I returned, to meet Jack, I confided our woes to him. One could tell Jack anything.

"You've got it wrong somehow," said Jack, "linking" me. "Come to Miss Lining's."

Miss Lining was our village dressmaker. A very bad one certainly, but still she could gore a skirt. She was not a native of the village, and signified her superior gentility by a mincing pronunciation. She had also a hiss with the sibilants peculiar to herself. Before I could remonstrate, Jack was knocking at the door.

"Good-afternoon, Miss Lining. Miss Margery has been making a dress, and she's got into a muddle with the gores. Now, how do you manage with gores, Miss Lining?" Jack confidentially inquired, taking his hat off, and accepting a well-dusted chair.

There was now nothing for it but to explain my difficulties, which I did, Miss Lining saying, "Yisss, misss," at every two or three words. When I had said my say, she sucked the top of her brass thimble thoughtfully for some moments, and then spoke as an oracle.

"There's a hinside and a hout to the stuff? Yisss, misss. And a hup and a down? Yisss, misss."

"And quite half the gores won't fit in anywhere," I desperately interposed.

Miss Lining took another taste of the brass thimble, and then said:

"In course, misss, with a patterned thing there's as many gores to throw hout as to huse. Yisss, misss."

"*Are there?*" said I. "But what a waste!"

"Ho no, misss! you cuts the body out of the gores you throws hout, misss——"

"Well, if you get the body out of them, there must be a waist!" Jack broke in, as he sat fondling Miss Lining's tom-cat.

"Ho no, sir!" said Miss Lining, who couldn't have seen a joke to save her dignity. "They cuts to good add-vantage, sir."

The mystery was now clear to me, and Jack saw this by my face.

"You understand?" said he briefly, setting down the cat.

"Quite," said I. "Our mistake was beginning with the bodies. But we can get some more stuff."

"An odd bit always comes in," said Miss Lining, speaking, I fear, from an experience of bits saved from the dresses of village patrons. "Yisss, misss."

"Well, good-afternoon, Miss Lining," said Jack, who never suffered, as Eleanor and I sometimes did, from a difficulty in getting away from a cottage. "Thank you very much. Have you heard from your sister at Buxton lately?"

"Last week, sir," said Miss Lining.

"And how is she?" said Jack urbanely.

He never forgot any one, and he never grudged sympathy—two qualities which made him beloved of the village.

"Quite well, thank you, sir, and the same to you," said Miss Lining, beaming; "except that she do suffer a deal in her inside, sir."

"Chamomile tea is very good for the inside, I believe," said Jack, putting on his hat with perfect gravity.

"So I've 'eerd—yisss, sir," said Miss Lining; "and there's something of the same in them pills that's spoke so well of in your magazine, sir, I think. I sent by the carrier for a box, sir, on Saturday last, and would have done sooner, but for waiting for Mrs. Barker to pay for the pelerine I made out of her uncle's funeral scarf. Yisss, misss."

Jack was very seldom at a loss, but on this occasion he seemed puzzled.

"Pills recommended in our magazine?" he said, as we strolled up towards the Vicarage. "It's those medical tracts you and Eleanor have been taking round lately."

"There's nothing about pills in them," said I. "They're about drains, and fresh air, and cleanliness. Besides, she said our magazine."

"We don't give them any magazine but the *Parishioner's Pennyworth* and the missionary one," said Jack. "I'm stumped, Margery."

But in a few minutes I was startled by his seizing me by the shoulders and leaning against me in a paroxysm of laughter.

"Oh, Margery, I've got it! It *is* the *Parishioner's Pennyworth.* There's been an advertisement at the end of it for months, like a fly-leaf, of Norton's chamomile pills."

And as I unravelled to Eleanor the mystery of our dressmaking difficulties, we could hear Jack convulsing Mrs. Arkwright with a perfect reproduction of Miss Lining's accent—"Them pills that's spoke so well of in your magazine. Yisss, m'm."

We got some more material, and finished the dresses triumphantly. By the next summer we were skilful enough to use our taste with some freedom and good success.

I was then fifteen, and in long dresses. I remember some most tasteful costumes which we produced; and as we contemplated them as they hung, flounced, furbelowed, and finished, upon pegs, Eleanor said:

"I wonder where we shall display these this year?"

How little we knew! We had made the dresses alike, to the nicety of a bow, because we thought it ladylike that the costumes of sisters should be so. How far we were from guessing that they would not be worn together after all!

CHAPTER XXVIII.

I GO BACK TO THE VINE—AFTER SUNSET—A TWILIGHT EXISTENCE—SALAD OF MONK'S-HOOD—A ROYAL SUMMONS.

The few marked events of my life have generally happened on my birthdays. It was on my fifteenth birthday that Mr. Arkwright got a letter from one of my relations on the subject of my going to live with my great-grandfather and grandmother.

They were now very old. My great-grandfather was becoming "childish," and the little dear duchess was old and frail for such a charge alone. They had no daughter. The religious question was laid aside. My most Protestant relatives thought my duty in the matter overwhelming, and with all my clinging of heart to the moor home I felt myself that it was so.

I don't know how I got over the parting. I wandered hopelessly about familiar spots, and wished I had made sketches of them; but how could I know I had not all life before me? The time was short, and preparations had to be made. This kept us quiet. At the last, Jack put in all my luggage, and did everything for me. Then he kissed me, and said, "God bless you, Margery," and "linking" Eleanor by force, led her away and comforted her like the good, dear boy he is. Clement drove me so recklessly down the steep hill, and over the stones, that the momentary expectation of an upset dried my tears, and I did not see much of the villagers' kind and too touching farewells.

And so to the bleak station again, and the familiar old porter, whom fate seems to leave long enough at *his* post, and on through the whirling railway panorama, by which one passes to so much joy and so much sorrow—and then I was at The Vine once more.

I wonder if I am like my great-grandmother in her youth? Some people (Elspeth among them) declare that it is so; and others that I am like my poor mother. I suppose I have some Vandaleur features, from an eerie little incident which befell me on the threshold of The Vine—an appropriate beginning to a life that always felt like a weird, shadowy dream.

I did not ring the bell of the outer gate on my arrival, because Adolphe (grown up, but with the old, ruddy boy's face on the top of his man's shoulders) was anxiously waiting for me, and devoted himself to my luggage, telling me that Master was in the garden. Thither I ran so hastily, that a straggling sweetbriar caught my hat and my net, and dragged them off, sending my hair over my shoulders. My hair is not long, however, like

Eleanor's, and it curls, and I sometimes wear it loose; so I did not stop to rearrange it, but hurried on towards my great-grandfather, who was coming slowly to meet me from the other end of the terrace, his hands behind his back, as of old. At least, I thought it was to meet me; but as he came near I saw that he was unconscious of my presence. He looked very old, his face was pale and shrivelled, like a crumpled white kid glove; his wild blue eyes, insensible of what was before them, seemed intently fixed on something that no one else could see, and he was talking to himself, as we call it when folk talk with the invisible.

It was very silly, but I really felt the colour fading from my face with fright. My great-grandfather's back was to the west, where a few bars of red across the sky, as it was to be seen through the Scotch firs, were all that remained of the sunset. That strange light was on everything, of which modern pre-Raphaelite painters are so fond. I was tired with my long journey and previous excitement; and when I suddenly remembered that Mr. Vandaleur was said to have in some measure lost his reason, a shudder came over me. In a moment more he saw me. I think my crimson cloak caught his eye, but his welcome was hardly less alarming than his abstraction. He started, and held up his hands, and a pained, puzzled expression troubled his face. Then a flush, which seemed to make him look older than the whiteness; and then, with a shrill, feeble cry of "Victoire, ma belle!" he tottered towards me so hastily that I thought he must have fallen; but, like a vision, a little figure flitted from the French window of the drawing-room, and in a moment my great-grandmother was supporting him, and soothing him with gentle words in French. I could see now how helpless he was. For a bit he seemed still puzzled and confused; but he clung to her and kissed her hand, and suffered himself to be led indoors. Then I followed them, through the window, into the room where the candles were not yet lighted for economy's sake—the glare of the red sunset bars making everything dark to me—with a strange sense of gloom.

It would be hard to imagine a stronger contrast than that between my life in my new home and my life in my home upon the moors. At the Arkwrights' we lived so essentially with the times. Our politics, on the whole, were liberal; our theology inclined to be broad; our ideas on social subjects were reformatory, progressive, experimental. Scientific subjects were a speciality of the household; and, living in a manufacturing district, mere neighbourhood kept us with the great current of mercantile interests. We argued each other into a general unfixity of opinions; and, full of youthful dreams of golden ages, were willing to believe this young world—where not yet we, but only our words could fly—to be but upon the threshold of true civilization. Above all, life seemed so short, our hands were so full, so over-full of work, the daylight was not long enough for us, and we grudged meals and sleep.

How different it was under the shadow of this old Vine! I am very thankful, now, that I had grace, under the sense of "wasted time," which was at first so irritating, to hold by my supreme child-duty towards my aged parents against the mere modern fuss of "work," against what John Wesley called the "lust of finishing" any labour, and to serve them in their way rather than in my own. But the change was very great. How we "pottered" through the days!—with what needless formalities, what slowness, what indecision! How fatiguing is enforced idleness! How lengthy were the evening meals, where we sat, trifling with the vine-leaves under a single dish of fruit, till the gloaming deepened into gloom!

At fifteen one is very susceptible of impressions; very impatient of what one is not used to. The very four-post bed in which I slept oppressed me, and the cracked basin held together for years by the circular hole in the old-fashioned washstand. The execution-picture only made me laugh now.

Then, as to the meals. No doubt a great many people eat and drink too much, as we are beginning to discover. Whether we at the Vicarage did, I cannot say; but the change to the unsubstantial fare on which very old people like the Vandaleurs keep the flickering light of life aglow was very great; and yet in this slow, vegetating existence my appetite soon died away. The country was flat and damp too; and by and by neuralgia kept me awake at night, as regularly as the ghost of my great-grandfather had done in years gone by. But it is strange how quickly unmarked time slips on. Day after day, week after week ran by, till a lassitude crept over me in which I felt amazed at former ambitions, and a certain facility of sympathy, which has been in many respects an evil, and in many a good to me, seemed to mould me to the interests of the fading household. And so I lived the life of my great-grandparents, which was as if science made no strides, and men no struggles; as if nothing were to be done with the days, but to wear through them in all patient goodness, loyal to a long-fallen dynasty, regretful of some ancient virtues and courtesies, tender towards past beauties and passions, and patient of succeeding sunsets, till this aged world should crumble to its close.

My great-grandfather came to know me again, though his mind was in a disordered, dreary condition; from old age, Elspeth said, but it often recalled what I had heard of the state of his mother's intellect before her death. The dear little old lady's intellects were quite bright, and, happily, not only entire, but cultivated. I do not know how people who think babies and servants are a woman's only legitimate interests would like to live with women who have either never met with, or long outlived them. I know how my dear granny's educated mind and sense of humour helped us over a dozen little domestic difficulties, and broke the neck of fidgets that seemed almost inevitable at her great age and in that confined sphere of interests.

I certainly faded in our twilight existence, as if there were some truth in the strange old theory that very aged people can withdraw vital force from young companions and live upon it. But every day and hour of my stay made me love and reverence my great-grandmother more and more, and be more and more glad that I had come to know her, and perhaps be of some little service to her.

Indeed, it was my great-grandfather's condition that kept us so much among the shadows. The old lady had a delightful youthfulness of spirit, and took an almost wistful pleasure in hearing about our life at the Arkwrights', as if some ambitious Scotch blood in her would fain have kept better pace with the currents of the busy world. But when my grandfather joined us, we had to change the subject. Modern ideas jarred upon him. And it was seldom that he was not with us. The tender love between the old couple was very touching.

"It must seem strange to you, my dear, to think of such long lives so little broken by events," said my great-grandmother. "But your dear grandfather and I have never been apart for a day since our happy marriage."

I do not think they were apart for an hour whilst I was with them. He followed her about the house, if she left him for many minutes, crying, "Victoire! Victoire!" chiefly from love, but I was sometimes spiteful enough to think also because he could not amuse himself.

"The master's calling for you again," said Elspeth, with some impatience, one day when grandmamma was teaching me a bit of dainty cookery in the kitchen.

"Oh, fly, petite!" she cried to me; "and say that his Majesty has summoned the Duchess."

Much bewildered, I ran out, and met my great-grandfather on the terrace, crying, "Victoire! Victoire!" in fretful tones.

"His Majesty has summoned the Duchess, sir," said I, dropping a slight curtsy, as I generally did on disturbing the old gentleman.

To my astonishment, this seemed quite to content him. He drew in his elbows, and spread the palms of his hands with a very polite bow, saying, "Bien, bien;" and after murmuring something else in French, which I did not catch, but which I fancy was an acknowledgment of the prior claims of royalty, he folded his hands behind his back and wandered away down the terrace, as I rushed off to my confectionery again.

I found that this use of the old fable, which had calmed my great-grandfather in past days, was no new idea. It was, in fact, a graceful fiction which deceived nobody, and had been devised by my great-grandmother out of deference to her husband's prejudices. In the long years when they were very poor, their poverty was made, not only tolerable but graceful, by Mrs. Vandaleur's untiring energy, but (though he wouldn't, or perhaps couldn't, find any occupation by which to add to their income) the sight of his Victoire, who should have been a duchess, doing any menial work so distracted him, that my grandmother had to devise some method to secure herself from his observation when she washed certain bits of priceless lace which redeemed her old dresses from commonness, or cooked some delicacy for Mons. le Duc's dinner, or mended his honourable clothes. Thus Jeanette's old fable came into use; first in jest, and then as an adopted form for getting rid of my great-grandfather when he was in the way. It must have astonished a practical woman like my great-grandmother to find how completely it satisfied him. But there must have been a time when his helplessness and impracticability tried her in many ways, before she fairly came to realize that he never could be changed, and her love fell in with his humours. On this point he was humoured completely, and never inquired on what business his deceased Majesty of France required the attendance of the Duchess that should have been!

To do him justice, if he was a helpless he was a very tender husband.

"He has never said a rude or unkind word to me since we were boy and girl together," said the little old lady, with tears in her eyes. And indeed, courtesy implies self-discipline; and even now the old man's politeness checked his petulance over and over again. He never gave up the habit of gathering flowers for my grandmother, and such exquisite contrasts of colour I never saw combined by any other hand. Another accomplishment of his was also connected with his love of plants.

"It's little enough a man can do about a house the best of times," said Elspeth, "and the master's just as feckless as a bairn. But he makes a fine sallet."

I shudder almost as I write the words. How little we thought that my poor grandfather's one useful gift would have so fatal an ending!

But I must put it down in order. It was the end of many things. Of my life at The Vine among them, and very nearly of my life in this world altogether. My great-grandfather made delicious salads. I have heard him say that he preferred our English habit of mixing ingredients to the French one of dressing one vegetable by itself; but he said we did not carry it far enough, we neglected so many useful herbs. And so his salads were compounded notonly of lettuce and cress, and so forth, but of dandelion, sorrel, and half-a-dozen other field or garden plants. Sometimes one flavour preponderated, sometimes another, and the sauce was always good.

Now it is all over it seems to me that I must have been very stupid not to have paid more attention to the strange flavour in the salad that day. But I was thinking chiefly of the old lady, who was not very well (Elspeth had an idea that she had had a very slight "stroke," but how this was we cannot know now), whilst my grandfather was almost flightily cheerful. I tasted the salad, and did not eat it, but I was the less inclined to complain of it as they seemed perfectly satisfied.

Then my grandmother was taken ill. At first we thought it a development of what we had noticed. Then Mr. Vandaleur became ill also, and we sent Adolphe in haste for the doctor. At last we found out the truth. The salad was full of young leaves of monk's-hood. Under what delusion my poor grandfather had gathered them we never knew. Elspeth and I were busy with the old lady, and he had made the salad without help from any one.

From the first the doctor gave us little hope, and they sank rapidly. Their priest, for whom Adolphe made a second expedition, did not arrive in time; they were in separate rooms, and Elspeth and I flitted from one to the other in sad attendance. The dear little old lady sank fast, and died in the evening.

Then the doctor impressed on us the necessity of keeping her death from my great-grandfather's knowledge.

"But supposing he asks?" said I.

"Say any soothing thing your ready wit may suggest, my dear young lady. But the truth, in his present condition, would be a fatal shock."

It haunted me. "Supposing he asks." And late in the evening he did ask! I was alone with him, and he called me.

"Marguerite, dear child, thou wilt tell me the truth. Why does my wife, my Victoire, thy grandmother, not come to me?"

Pondering what lie I could tell him, and how, an irresistible impulse seized me. I bent over him and said:

"Dear sir, the King has summoned the Duchess."

Does the mind regain power as the body fails? My great-grandfather turned his head, and, as his blue eyes met mine, I could not persuade myself that he was deceived.

"The will of his Majesty be done," he said faintly but firmly.

The next few moments seemed like years. Had I done wrong? Had it done him harm? Above all, what did he mean? Were his words part of one last graceful dream of the dynasty of the white lilies, or was his loyal submission made now to a Majesty not of France, not even of this world? It was an intense relief to me when he spoke again.

"Marguerite!"

I knelt by the bedside, and he laid his hand upon my head. An exquisite smile shone on his face.

"Good child; pauvre petite! His Majesty will call me also, before long. Is it not so? And then thou shalt rest."

His fine face clouded again with a wandering, troubled look, and his fingers fumbled the bed-clothes. I saw that he had lost his crucifix in moving his hand to my head. I gave it him, and he clasped his hands over it once more, and carrying it to his lips with a smile, closed his eyes like some good child going to sleep.

And Thou, O King of kings, didst summon him, as the dark faded into dawn!

CHAPTER XXIX.

HOME AGAIN—HOME NEWS—THE VERY END.

Now it is past it seems like a dream, my life at The Vine, with its sad end, if indeed that can be justly called a sad end which took away together, and with little pain, those dear souls whose married life had not known the parting of a day, and who in death were not (even by a day) divided.

And so I went back to the moors. I was weak and ill when I started, but every breath of air on my northward journey seemed to bring me strength.

There are no events in that porter's life, I am convinced. He looked just the same, and took me and my boxes quite coolly, though I felt inclined to shake hands with him in my delight. I did cry for very joy as we toiled up the old sandy hill, and the great moors welcomed me back. Then came the church, then the Vicarage, with the union-jack out of my window, and the villagers were at their doors—and I was at home. Oh, how the dear boys tore me to pieces!

There was no very special news, it seemed. Clement had been very good in taking my class at school, and had established a cricket club. Jack had positively found a new fungus, which would probably be named after him. "Boy's luck," as we all said! Captain Abercrombie had been staying with an old uncle at a place close by, only about twelve miles off. And he was constantly driving over. "So very good-natured to the boys," Mr. Arkwright said. And there was to be a school-children's tea on my birthday.

My birthday has come and gone, and I am sixteen now. Dear old Eleanor and I have gone back to our old ways. She had left my side of our room untouched. It was in talking of our recent parting, and all that has come and gone in our lives, that the fancy came upon us of writing our biographies this winter.

And here, in the dear old kitchen, round which the wild wind howls like music, with the dear boys dreaming at our feet, we bring them to an end.

* * * * * *

This dusty relic of an old fad had been lying by for more than a year, when I found it to-day, in emptying a box to send some books in to Oxford, to Jack.

Eleanor should have had it, for we are parted, after all; but her husband has more interest in hers, so we each keep our own.

She is married, to George Abercrombie, and I mean to paste the bit out of the newspaper account of their wedding on to the end of this, as a sort of last chapter. It would be as long as all the rest put together if I were to write down all the ups and downs, and ins and outs, that went before the marriage, and I suppose these things are always very much alike.

I like him very much, and I am going to stay with them. The wedding was very pretty. Jack threw shoes to such an extent, that when I went to change my white ones I couldn't find a complete pair to put on. He says he meant to pick them up again, but Prince, our new puppy, thought they were thrown for him, and he never brought them back. Dear boy!

The old uncle helps George, who I believe is his heir, but at present he sticks to the regiment. It seems so funny that Eleanor should now be living there, and I here. In her letter to-day she says: "Fancy, Margery, my having quarrelled with Mrs. Minchin and not known it! She called on me to-day and solemnly forgave me, whereby I learned that she had been 'cutting' me for six weeks. When she said, 'No doubt you thought it very strange, Mrs. Abercrombie, that I never called on your mother whilst she was with you,' I was obliged to get over it the best way I could, for I dare not tell her I had never noticed it. I think my offence was something about calls, and I must be more particular. But George and I have been sketching at every spare moment this lovely weather. Oh, Margery dear, I do often feel so thankful to my mother for having given us plenty of rational interests. I could really imagine even *our* quarrelling or getting tired of each other, if we had nothing but ourselves in common. As it is, you can't tell, till you have a husband of your own, what a double delight there is in everything we do together. As to social ups and downs, and not having much money or many fine dresses, a 'collection' alone makes one almost too indifferent. Do you remember Mother's saying long ago, that intellectual pleasures have this in common with the consolations of religion, that they are such as the world can neither give nor take away?"

THE END.

Richard Clay & Sons, Limited, London & Bungay.

The present Series of Mrs. Ewing's Works is the only authorized, complete, and uniform Edition published.

It will consist of 18 volumes, Small Crown 8vo, at 2s. 6d. per vol., issued, as far as possible, in chronological order, and these will appear at the rate of two volumes every two months, so that the Series will be completed within 18 months. The device of the cover was specially designed by a Friend of Mrs. Ewing.

The following is a list of the books included in the Series—

1. MELCHIOR'S DREAM, AND OTHER TALES.
2. MRS. OVERTHEWAY'S REMEMBRANCES.
3. OLD-FASHIONED FAIRY-TALES.
4. A FLAT IRON FOR A FARTHING.
5. THE BROWNIES, AND OTHER TALES.
6. SIX TO SIXTEEN.
7. LOB-LIE-BY-THE-FIRE, AND OTHER TALES.
8. JAN OF THE WINDMILL.
9. VERSES FOR CHILDREN, AND SONGS.
10. THE PEACE EGG—A CHRISTMAS MUMMING PLAY—HINTS FOR PRIVATE THEATRICALS, &c.
11. A GREAT EMERGENCY, AND OTHER TALES.
12. BROTHERS OF PITY, AND OTHER TALES OF BEASTS AND MEN.
13. WE AND THE WORLD, Part I.
14. WE AND THE WORLD, Part II.
15. JACKANAPES—DADDY DARWIN'S DOVE-COTE—THE STORY OF A SHORT LIFE.
16. MARY'S MEADOW, AND OTHER TALES OF FIELDS AND FLOWERS.
17. MISCELLANEA, including The Mystery of the Bloody Hand—Wonder Stories—Tales of the Khoja, and other translations.
18. JULIANA HORATIA EWING AND HER BOOKS, with a selection from Mrs. Ewing's Letters.

Lightning Source UK Ltd.
Milton Keynes UK
UKHW040715221222
414324UK00004B/519

9 783734 060724